The last gu
odds had been narrowed

The gangbanger raised his gun and sprayed indiscriminately in the warrior's direction. Bolan took cover and grimaced at the thought that an innocent bystander might get in the way.

Unfortunately for the gun-toting hood, he'd never have the chance to kill Bolan or a noncombatant.

The man's body began to rock under the impact of the half-dozen or so police weapons suddenly aimed at him. The cops doled out a fury of destructive automatic fire from their Colt AR-15s and pistols. The thug staggered a moment and then collapsed to the pavement.

Bolan continued in motion around the corner and sprinted down the street. He would have to lay low for a while, come back later to retrieve his vehicle. He couldn't spend the next twenty-four hours in a police lockup under interrogation. He still had a lot to do in Phoenix.

The mission had only just begun.

MACK BOLAN ®

The Executioner

The
Executioner®
Don Pendleton's

RECOVERY FORCE

A GOLD EAGLE BOOK FROM
W RLDWIDE®

TORONTO • NEW YORK • LONDON
AMSTERDAM • PARIS • SYDNEY • HAMBURG
STOCKHOLM • ATHENS • TOKYO • MILAN
MADRID • WARSAW • BUDAPEST • AUCKLAND

Recycling programs
for this product may
not exist in your area.

First edition December 2010

ISBN-13: 978-0-373-64385-1

Special thanks and acknowledgment to
Jon Guenther for his contribution to this work.

RECOVERY FORCE

Printed in U.S.A.

The law condemns and punishes only actions within certain definite and narrow limits; it thereby justifies, in a way, all similar actions that lie outside those limits.

—Leo Tolstoy
1828–1910
What I Believe

I won't stand by and watch this epidemic of terror spread throughout America. As long as I have breath in me, I will stamp out these kidnappers, murderers and drug peddlers at the source.

—Mack Bolan

THE
MACK BOLAN

LEGEND

Nothing less than a war could have fashioned the destiny of the man called Mack Bolan. Bolan earned the Executioner title in the jungle hell of Vietnam.

But this soldier also wore another name—Sergeant Mercy. He was so tagged because of the compassion he showed to wounded comrades-in-arms and Vietnamese civilians.

Mack Bolan's second tour of duty ended prematurely when he was given emergency leave to return home and bury his family, victims of the Mob. Then he declared a one-man war against the Mafia.

He confronted the Families head-on from coast to coast, and soon a hope of victory began to appear. But Bolan had broken society's every rule. That same society started gunning for this elusive warrior—to no avail.

So Bolan was offered amnesty to work within the system against terrorism. This time, as an employee of Uncle Sam, Bolan became Colonel John Phoenix. With a command center at Stony Man Farm in Virginia, he and his new allies—Able Team and Phoenix Force—waged relentless war on a new adversary: the KGB.

But when his one true love, April Rose, died at the hands of the Soviet terror machine, Bolan severed all ties with Establishment authority.

Now, after a lengthy lone-wolf struggle and much soul-searching, the Executioner has agreed to enter an "arm's-length" alliance with his government once more, reserving the right to pursue personal missions in his Everlasting War.

"We're in the eye of the storm. If it doesn't stop here, if we're not able to fix it here and get it turned around, it will go across the nation."

—Chief of Police
Phoenix, Arizona

I won't stand by and watch this epidemic of terror spread throughout America. As long as I have breath in me, I will stamp out these kidnappers, murderers and drug peddlers at the source.

—Mack Bolan, The Executioner

Prologue

The girl awoke with a start, covered in sweat.

Her heart thumped in her chest; her breath came in short bursts—more like gasping than breathing. She tried to reach up to the pain at the back of her head that throbbed with each beat of her heart. In her state of murky consciousness, it took time to realize that someone had bound her hands....

SHE DIDN'T REMEMBER passing out but realized she must have because she came to again with much the same reaction. She noticed her parched throat this time and it felt as if her tongue had swollen to twice its normal size. She wanted to puke but she realized if she did it could mean death. The gag would prevent her from voiding and she might choke on her own vomit. So she wretched a few times and swallowed back anything more.

Only fourteen years of age, she hadn't known such terror before and probably wouldn't know it again.

Then she thought of her boyfriend, Dino Montera, only two years older than her. He was a tall kid, muscular and in good shape, a football player on the junior varsity team. Even Dino had been caught off guard by the men who seemed to come out of nowhere. At least, Ann-Elise *thought* that they were men, although she sort of remembered hearing a woman's voice at some point, too. The only other thing she could remember was that they spoke in another language, probably Spanish. Maybe Spanish? Ann-Elise couldn't be really sure, but she would have to pay better attention because the cops would want to know when they came to her rescue.

Then she looked over to her right, turning her head slowly to stave off the pain. She remembered, as she stared at her boyfriend through blurred vision—poor Dino was tied to a chair, his face blood-caked—that something had struck her in the back of the head. Hard. That's why it probably hurt so much. God, maybe she had brain damage or something. She'd heard about that kind of thing happening after being hit in the head. And Ann-Elise knew about those things because she'd studied them in her dad's medical books. One day, she wanted to be a doctor, like her dad.

Her mother, a prominent attorney to residents of Scottsdale, had warned her not to go gallivanting about downtown Phoenix without an adult. What difference would that have made? If the men who had knocked her unconscious were able to take down a young man Dino's size, they would have been able to take down any adult just as easily.

Ann-Elise didn't have to wonder anymore about her captors because one of them suddenly appeared, blocking her line of sight. She looked up at the man but he'd concealed his face with some sort of mask. She couldn't really make out anything about him other than he was *very* big, and he had dark eyes. There wasn't any emotion in them. They stared at her without pity or consideration, and Ann-Elise considered in that moment the horrific possibility they might hurt her more. Ann-Elise decided not to think about such things yet. Obviously, they had kidnapped her and Dino for ransom and she knew her father and mother had enough money to pay. They would pay her captors, pay whatever it took. And they had many wealthy friends, too. They lived in a city that was home to some of the wealthiest people in the world. At least, that's what everyone at the academy said.

Boy, she wouldn't be able to live this one down.

The man stared at her another moment and then turned his attention to Dino. Ann-Elise watched with a mixed sense of shock and terror as the man reached down to grab something and came up with a large, plastic bucket. He suddenly heaved the bucket in Dino's direction and doused him with water. Probably cold water.

The bastard!

Dino came suddenly awake and choked back what sounded like a scream. The man stood there a moment, arms folded, and Ann-Elise thought she heard him make a noise. Something that sounded like a laugh. Then the man reached forward suddenly, untied Dino and hauled him out of the chair. Dino staggered and stumbled around like a drunk, and Ann-Elise realized he'd probably put up more of a fight than she had, so they had to beat him up to stop him. Her poor, poor Dino. He had taken punishment intended for her just because he tried to protect her.

The man finally clamped a hand on Dino's shoulder and steered him out of Ann-Elise's sight. She began to make protests, screaming against the gag and warning the man with a flurry of threats and curses not to hurt her boyfriend, but she couldn't see if it had any effect. Not that she thought it would…. She began to cry, trying to refrain because that made it more difficult to breathe. Her cries became sobs as she heard an incessant thumping noise—a sound that could only have been Dino taking another beating.

Why were they hurting him? What had he done to them?

Her mind screamed at them to stop but she knew she could do nothing about it.

And then for a long time the sounds stopped and she heard no more noise, nothing. Then the sound of voices, angry voices arguing or something.

Yes, it was definitely Spanish.

Then she heard a door open and the man came back into view, walking backward and dragging something, but Ann-Elise couldn't tell what. Although she knew it was probably Dino, she didn't want to think about it. Maybe not. Maybe it was just some equipment, a bag or box or something. Whatever it was, the man wasn't too gentle about dumping the load onto the floor next to her. The man didn't give her a glance as he stomped out and slammed the door behind him, causing Ann-Elise to jump.

And she began to cry again, moaning Dino's name past the gag, the sound of her cries muffled in her own ears.

Mack Bolan lowered the binoculars and frowned. Too quiet.

He sat in his vehicle parked a half block from the residence where he believed members of the Sinaloa drug cartel were holding a teenage girl and her boyfriend. The sun beat through the windshield, threatening to roast him out. All windows were down and the sunroof open to facilitate air movement, but there didn't seem to be much of it today in southwest Phoenix. So Bolan sat practically motionless and ignored the heavy sweat that soaked his face, neck and areas where his clothing fit snugly.

The warrior looked a bit out of place.

Although he'd dressed like a native in khaki-style shorts and a loose-fitting polo, it still looked idiotic for him to be sitting in his car in the midmorning heat. Fortunately, activity in the neighborhood had seemed minimal, most everyone already having gone to work or run the day's errands. Bolan had been sitting there since about 0730 hours and it was nearing eleven.

There hadn't been so much as a stirring around or in the target house. The shades were pulled and only a dusty, early-model SUV sat in the drive. Bolan scanned the place one more time through the binoculars, then studied the black-and-white print made from a yearbook photo of the missing girl, and a similar one taken around the same time of her boyfriend.

The Executioner's intelligence had been sketchy, but he knew the information provided by Stony Man would be much more solid than anything the Phoenix police could give him. Trouble had come to the Sun City and it seemed nobody could do anything about it. Half the country believed the press when they touted the war between the Sinaloa and Gulf drug cartels out of Mexico as the primary reason for the rise in kidnappings. The other half chalked it up to nothing more than media hype. The naysayers were convinced the kidnappings were mostly related to the higher likelihood ransoms would be paid due to the fact Arizona had long attracted the rich and elite.

Bolan thought both sides of the issue had merit. But with the numbers at an all-time high, the Executioner realized the time had come to put an end to it. And while he couldn't completely eliminate it, the problem was large enough that it could branch out. The best way to stop it was here and now—terminate the enemy's plan of action before it reached that point.

And Bolan planned to start with two innocent teenagers.

Bolan put the photos away, secured the binoculars and then checked the action on his .44 Magnum Desert Eagle. The pistol had served him well on many past missions, and recently he'd upgraded to the newer Mark XIX model with a brushed chrome finish. The Beretta 93-R that he normally wore in shoulder leather rode in a hip holster concealed by the loose-fit polo. His best offense would be surprise, in this instance, since the place wasn't likely to be heavily fortified or guarded. Additionally, the Sinaloa cartel had probably been using it as a stash house for a while, which means any of its occupants would be relaxed and not too alert. That made it a perfect target for someone with the Executioner's special talents.

Bolan laid the Desert Eagle on the passenger seat, started the rental car and coasted down the street until he came within a few yards. He then swung the nose into the driveway at an angle as he picked up speed and drove across the pavement onto the lawn of half-dead grass. When he got within a few feet of the front door he gave the horn a blast before snatching up the pistol and going EVA.

Less than a minute elapsed before the door opened and a stocky, bare-chested Mexican with a shaved head and tattoos covering half his body emerged from the house. He looked angry as he gave the sedan a once-over, but then his eyes tracked to the right. But he was too late and Bolan was on him before the hood could react in time to bring up the pistol he'd been holding behind his baggy jeans. Bolan caught him with a kick that broke several ribs and drove the cartel gangster into the unyielding metal of the foreign-make rental. As the guy's body bounced off of it, Bolan followed with a backhand that drove the butt of his pistol into a point behind his opponent's ear. The guy dropped to the pavement like a stone.

Bolan pushed through the front door in time to see another hood emerge from a hallway off the main living area. The man raised a pistol, holding it gangster style with the ejector port pointed up. Bolan snap-aimed the Desert Eagle and squeezed the trigger twice. Happenstance favored Bolan because that first round struck the gunman's hand that held the pistol and sent it flying. The second round landed dead-center in the chest, fracturing the breastbone before coring through tissue to the spine and driving the hood into the wall behind him. He collapsed on the carpet in a heap.

Another gunner jumped into view, framed by an entryway into the kitchen, a shotgun in his hand. Bolan dove in time to avoid the first blast of buckshot that winged over his body and blew a massive hole in the drywall. The warrior rolled and that saved him from a second blast into the carpet that sent dust, dirt and chunks of crushed carpet fibers in every direction. Bolan followed through the roll and into a firing posture on one knee. He acquired his target in milliseconds and triggered a round before the man could get off a third shot. The 280-gram slug busted through the hood's left side, perforating his heart as it traveled upward at an angle and exited out his right armpit. The impact spun the enemy and he slammed against the wall. The shotgun clattered to the linoleum followed by the corpse a heartbeat later.

Bolan swept the muzzle of the Desert Eagle across his immediate field of fire, eyes and ears attuned to any further threats. Eventually, he relaxed and got to his feet, although he didn't let down his guard. He held the .44 Magnum at a ready state while he scoured the rest of the house. Eventually, he found a door concealing a stairwell that emerged onto a semifinished basement.

The sight of a breathing, conscious girl tied to an old table sent a ripple of satisfaction through Bolan's tired body, but he also noticed the lump of bruised, beaten flesh on the ground. He rushed to the boy's motionless form and checked the pulse at the neck. Nothing. Bolan pressed his lips together in a hard mask as he rose and approached the girl.

"It's okay," he said as quietly and evenly as he could manage. "You're going to be all right, now. I'm not going to hurt you. Okay?"

She nodded, blinking those red-streaked crystal-blue eyes hard—she'd obviously been crying.

Bolan disposed of the gag that had left red welts across her cheeks and then cut away her bonds with a pocketknife version of the Cold Steel Tanto fighting knife. She choked and wheezed at first, and he watched her with concern. The moment proved short-lived and only Bolan's reflexes saved his tennis shoes from being covered by the significant amount of vomit she projected over the side of the table.

When it seemed she was finished and left only with dry heaves, Bolan said, "You don't look much like your yearbook photo."

She eyed him with a queer expression as he helped her sit up.

Bolan continued with a smile, "You're much prettier in person. I assume you're Ann-Elise?"

She nodded and wiped the side of her mouth. Her voice cracked when she said, "Dino? Is Dino okay?"

The warrior wished she would have asked him anything but that, although he knew it wasn't as if he could put off the subject indefinitely. Despite the trauma through which she'd gone, the young girl deserved to know the truth no matter how painful it might be. Until she could come to terms with his death, the healing could not begin.

"I'm sorry," Bolan whispered. "He didn't make it."

Ann-Elise looked at Bolan a moment and then let out a blood-curdling scream and threw her arms around him. He decided it was time for them to get the hell out of there, and he hauled her off the table and up the stairs without another look at Montera's corpse.

Once they were outside, Bolan seat-belted Ann-Elise into the passenger seat of the sedan and then ran around and climbed behind the wheel. He cranked the engine, backed off the lawn and onto the road, then proceeded at a conservative pace down the quiet street. He could have just as easily left in a display of screeching, smoking tires but he figured there was little point in drawing attention. The street still looked relatively deserted and he didn't detect the approach of police sirens.

That meant the commotion inside had probably gone unnoticed.

Good, he needed to buy some time. It wouldn't help his mission to risk unplanned contact with the police so early in the game. He had to get on the other side of the blue wall, sure, but on *his* terms. Anything less would only create more problems for him, more things to worry about.

Bolan had chosen to take this one on his own. At Stony Man Farm, Hal Brognola and Barbara Price were preoccupied with larger matters. Bolan had it on good authority from pilot Jack Grimaldi, that both the Phoenix Force and Able Team units were on assignments of a grave nature. So what else was new? Bolan thought about the battle-hardened veterans of Stony Man taking it to the enemy—he wished them well.

So yeah, he would go it alone this time.

Ann-Elise simply sobbed and curled her arms around herself. Bolan had rolled up the windows so the winds wouldn't buffet her as he pulled onto the highway. She didn't say anything to him and he didn't press it. He'd saved her from what would certainly have been a long and brutal captivity. That's what he did best, and he'd leave the social work and other similar services to those better qualified to render it.

In under thirty minutes, Bolan had arrived at the large home in a peaceful, residential section on the west side of Scottsdale, close to where it bordered Phoenix.

Bolan got out of the car, opened the door and unbuckled the seat belt. He offered a hand, but the girl chose to exit without assistance. She started to walk up the sidewalk to the door and then looked back at Bolan, who stood there with arms folded as he watched her.

"Go on, Ann-Elise. Go home, your family's waiting for you."

"You're—" She bit off the reply and seemed to chew uncertainly at her lip. When she took a deep breath she appeared to have mustered whatever courage it seemed to take to speak to him. "You're not coming?"

Bolan shook his head. "There would be questions. Too many for me to answer at this moment. Do you understand?"

"Funny," the girl replied with a slightly wistful smile. "But I guess I do."

Bolan nodded, winked and then got in the sedan and drove away.

AFTER DROPPING OFF Ann-Elise McCormack, Bolan returned to his hotel to clean up a bit.

He showered, changed into lightweight cotton slacks and

a black muscle shirt. He then transferred the Beretta 93-R to shoulder leather before donning a buttoned maroon shirt to conceal it. After cleaning the Desert Eagle and stowing it in his equipment bag, Bolan sifted through the yellow pages of the phone book until he found the address of a pharmacy on Phoenix's southwest side. He memorized the address and then stuffed the equipment bag under the bed, leaving the privacy tag on the outside of the door to wave off maid service.

The Executioner considered his options as he drove across town. He'd approach this part of his mission with a soft probe, at first. Bolan had intel the pharmacy was a Sinaloa cartel front for laundering drug money. A narco-military unit known as Los Negros provided protection and enforcement for Sinaloa cartel ops according to Bolan's DEA connection, Vince Gagliardi. Officially, Gagliardi was breaking every rule in the book by revealing anything he learned to Bolan. He'd been working deep undercover within the local drug distribution network as a low-ranking mule. Gagliardi had been building a case against Los Negros for some time by infiltrating Los Zetas, chief enforcement and operations for the competing Gulf cartel.

At their secret rendezvous in a Flagstaff coffee shop three days earlier, Gagliardi told Bolan, "Phoenix P.D. hadn't been able to gather enough evidence to hit the place until now."

"And why's that?" Bolan asked.

"Los Negros is an extremely efficient organization," Gagliardi said. "They're well-equipped and highly mobile. You see, after the Mexican army brought down Osiel Cárdonas in 2003, the Sinaloa cartel saw their opportunity to move into the Nuevo Laredo region. You familiar with that?"

Bolan nodded. Nuevo Laredo had always been the hotbed of activity in the war between the Sinaloa and Gulf cartels. The region had become an extremely important drug corridor. Nearly half of all drug exports from Mexico were smuggled through the area connected on the south side of the Rio Grande with Laredo, Texas. It seemed almost ironic the area had been nicknamed *la puerta a Mexico,* or the door to Mexico. If anything, Nuevo Laredo had definitely become that for the drug runners.

"Okay, so everybody inside knows that Edgar Valdez Villareal runs Los Negros, but the guy who's pulling the strings behind the move into Phoenix is a dude by the name of Hector Casco." Gagliardi surreptitiously slid a folder across the table and then lit a cigarette while Bolan glanced through various documents. "That contains a copy of his dossier and all the shit I could dredge up on him inside our computer files. Some of it was a little tough to come by because he's actively under investigation and there are things for which I don't have clearance."

"I appreciate it," Bolan said with a nod.

Indeed he did because despite the fact Bolan had saved Gagliardi from certain death once, the DEA man was once again putting his career *and* his life on the line. If anyone inside the Gulf cartel suspected betrayal and put a tail on him, Gagliardi wouldn't last twelve hours after leaving that coffee shop, never mind the heat he'd take if his handler found out he'd broken protocol to help out a friend and outsider. And the Executioner fit both those descriptors.

"What's Casco's angle?"

Gagliardi shrugged. "I can't be sure yet, but I think he's vying for the favorite-son position in this part of the border states. Maybe looking to become independent, as it were."

"That would make sense. If Casco can gain sole control of the pipeline from Nogales to Phoenix, he'd have an operation equal to or even exceeding the one out of Nuevo Laredo."

"Right," Gagliardi said. "But now the Home Invasion and Kidnapping Enforcement squad within the Phoenix P.D. has obtained information about this pharmacy. Word has it that a major meet is scheduled there three days from today. And according to everything I can gather this HIKE squad plans to be there for it. There's even talk Casco's going to make a personal appearance."

"Yeah. But for what reason?" Bolan said. "If your intelligence is good, they wouldn't risk such a meeting without some purpose."

"That I can't tell you," Gagliardi said. "But I can tell you my intel comes from pretty high up. I'd be very surprised if this wasn't the real thing."

Bolan had nodded in understanding. He couldn't bring himself to doubt the information because Gagliardi had risked a lot to get it to him. It also made some sense in that it appeared Hector Casco was out to make a name for himself; Casco obviously wanted a larger cut of the action if nothing else. Those two facts alone made it important enough to check out. Bolan's only choice, then, would be to do a soft probe of the place and see what turned up.

With Ann-Elise McCormack out of danger, Bolan felt the time had come to explore this a bit further. By this point, the police would be at the cartel residence on the other side of town in force, not to mention swarming the McCormack and Montera homes. That left the field wide open and bought Bolan a little more time to check out Gagliardi's intelligence.

Bolan pulled his vehicle into the back parking lot of a diner positioned directly across from the corner pharmacy. He stepped into the cool interior, sat down and ordered a sandwich. As he waited, the warrior studied the facade. The place looked plain, unremarkable really, save for the striped awnings that jutted from above the pair of large plate-glass windows—one each facing the cross streets. That old-fashioned look seemed out of place in this kind of "upscale" neighborhood and yet Bolan saw some wisdom in that. It made it seem like another friendly, neighborhood drugstore, maybe something out of Norman Rockwell.

Then the glint of light catching on metal from the rooftop of the three-story building across the street caught Bolan's eye. He watched with interest, never taking his eyes from the building save for a brief acknowledgement of the waitress, who set the plate on the table with a clank.

"Can I get you anything else, honey?" she asked, tossing her blond hair as she cracked her gum.

By the time Bolan answered her, he'd spotted a second rooftop enemy position and three more at street level. "There a pay phone around here?"

She nodded. "Out back."

Bolan held up a ten as he slid out of the booth and said, "Keep the change."

"Wow, a whole dollar-twenty-five," the waitress said with mock admiration. "Thanks, *sir.* Hey! What about your sandwich?"

But Bolan was already out the door and walking casually along the side of the building. He could have called from his cell phone but he didn't want any of the diner occupants to overhear him. Beside the fact, the pay phone would be at least a bit more secure for Gagliardi. If anyone traced the call to the undercover agent's own mobile phone, at least they wouldn't be able to tie it to anything solid.

Gagliardi answered on the first ring. "Yeah?"

"It's me," Bolan replied. "Can you talk?"

"At the moment. What's up?"

"You said the other day that rumor control had it Casco was going to be at this meet."

"Right."

"Any idea what time it was planned for?"

"Not a clue. I only know it was supposed to go down today."

"You know how to reach this guy who's heading up the HIKE squad?"

"Nope, but I got a name."

"What is it?"

"Captain Joseph Hall. Why?"

"Because I think he and his team are about to walk into a trap," Bolan replied.

2

No sooner had the words left the Executioner's mouth than he heard the squeal of tires on pavement.

He bid Gagliardi a hasty farewell, then skirted the building until he reached the corner and risked a glance in the direction of the pharmacy. Two unmarked units had arrived and parked on the sidewalk, flanked by two uniform squads blocking the intersection. A large police van arrived a moment later, probably dispatched to haul away whomever the cops took into custody.

Bolan whipped the Beretta from his shoulder holster and dashed along the side of the diner until the first rooftop sentry he'd spotted came into view. The warrior had only seconds to take the guy down before the sentry started sniping at the cops. He was packing SJHPs, subsonic to suppress noise, but at only 125-grain apiece it would also severely limit the chances for a first-hit kill. Bolan thumbed the selector to 3-round-burst mode. He then sighted on the shadowy figure visible just above the parapet and squeezed the trigger. A trio of 9 mm Parabellum rounds hit home, one striking the rifle mounted to a bipod while the other two slammed into the sentry's head. The guy dropped from sight in a red spray brightened by the blazing midday sun.

The muzzle of Bolan's 93-R attended the second rooftop position but he found it vacant. Either the sniper there had seen Bolan moving or he'd gone to alert the others at the arrival of Hall's squad.

Bolan turned his attention to the three ground-level heavies. One of them was using the door of a black SUV for cover as he sighted down the barrel of an assault rifle. From that vantage point, Bolan couldn't tell what kind of rifle it was but he knew that mattered very little. The gunner could intend only one thing and if he had enough guts to level a rifle at the police in broad daylight on a busy street, he sure as hell had the guts to use it.

Bolan didn't plan to give him that chance. He dashed across the street in the direction of the cops massed outside the front doors of the pharmacy and prepared to make tactical entry. Bolan sighted down the slide of the pistol and triggered a 3-round burst on the run. He nearly reached the sidewalk before triggering a second and then a third. None of the rounds hit but they came close enough to distract the hood holding the rifle. The staccato of autofire echoed through the air as the rounds went high and wide of the cloistered cops.

Bolan leaped onto the sidewalk as he dropped a clip into his palm, pocketed it and slammed home a fresh one. He body-checked an older, white-haired guy donned in a Kevlar vest. The impact sent the cop into one of his colleagues who was suited in full tactical gear just as a fresh volley of rounds chewed up the wall where the cop had been standing a moment earlier.

Bolan ignored the cops who shouted at him and turned their weapons, instead rolling away from them and coming up behind the grill of the police van. Bolan skirted around it and pressed toward the position of the guy yielding the rifle. The shooter still hadn't seemed to notice Bolan—he acted like the cops had spotted him and were shooting back—so the Executioner's fast approach went unchecked. By the time the hood realized his mistake Bolan had drawn close enough he couldn't miss. And he didn't. A trio of rounds perforated the man's left chest, cutting through heart and lungs with a fury. The man's rifle clattered to the pavement and he staggered backward under the impact, blood flowing freely from not only the wounds, but also the corners of his mouth. The enemy gunner, appearing to be a man of twenty or twenty-one, dropped to the ground and expired with a shudder.

By that time, the cops realized Bolan wasn't shooting at *them* and that their real enemy had sprung an ambush that the Executioner, friend or foe, seemed bent on putting to rest before the party got wound up. And by all accounts it looked to them like the warrior was doing a damned good job of it.

Bolan swung the muzzle of the Beretta 93-R until he acquired target number two in his sights and delivered another volley of slugs. While they might have been subsonic, the rounds did the job of neutralizing the gunman. The guy triggered a burst skyward before dropping his weapon and hitting a wall. He fell in almost slow motion, his eyes wide open in a vacant expression of death as blood seeped from the third eye left by one of Bolan's rounds.

The last gunner saw that within a moment the odds had been narrowed by two-thirds, and it didn't look like he stood much of a chance against the Executioner *and* the cops. He decided to take his chances with Bolan. He believed he could take this guy—he had the firepower and the guts. The hood raised his machine pistol, an older-model mini-Uzi, and sprayed in the direction of Bolan indiscriminately. The Executioner took cover and grimaced at the off-chance an innocent bystander might get in the way.

Unfortunately for the gun-toting hood, he'd never have the chance to kill Bolan or a noncombatant.

The man's body began to rock under the impact of the half-dozen or so police weapons suddenly aimed at him. The cops doled out a fury of destructive autofire from their Colt

AR-15s and pistols. The thug staggered a moment and then collapsed to the pavement.

Bolan continued in motion around the corner and sprinted down the street. He would have to lie low for a while, come back later to retrieve his vehicle. The warrior knew he still needed to make contact with Joseph Hall, but he had to do it on his own time and his own way. For the moment they would only try to apprehend Bolan, and the Executioner didn't feel like spending the next twenty-four hours in a police lockup under interrogation. He still had a lot to do in Phoenix.

The mission had only just begun.

JOE HALL, CAPTAIN OF the Home Invasion and Kidnapping Enforcement squad, stared with angst at the mess of bodies strewn along the streets of downtown Phoenix.

This was *his* city, and the mysterious stranger who had saved his life managed to disappear without a trace. No, the raid on the pharmacy hadn't gone as planned. They had five corpses, all of whom Hall assumed would eventually be tied back to affiliations with either a local street gang or Los Negros. In spite of the sudden change in plans, they had managed to round up everyone inside the pharmacy, a total of three employees and one manager, but he didn't think anything would come of it. They had no evidence of wrongdoing on the parts of any of the pharmacy workers, and all of the bad guys, any one of whom he *might* have coerced into talking, were all deceased.

Sergeant Larry Murach joined Hall as he stood over one of the dead. The coroner had arrived quickly enough and at least managed to get the bodies covered. It wasn't as if Hall cared much about protecting their dignity, but dead was still dead and it helped cut down the number of free gapers. A large crowd had formed but with the place taped off and the backup on scene, the uniforms were doing a pretty good job of keeping the looky-loos and press hounds at bay.

"What do you have?" Hall asked Murach, not taking his eyes off the covered body.

"Not much," Murach said, flipping through the couple of small pages of notes he'd taken. "All four of the deceased are gangbangers. Two actually have some ink that marks them as members of Los Negros, the other two are wearing colors but nothing else."

"Witnesses?"

"Nobody I talked to is really sure what the hell happened. I guess whoever saw these guys decided to stay healthy by giving them a wide berth."

And the only man with enough smarts to have spotted them ahead of time somehow managed to slip through our fingers, Hall thought. "What about our mystery man?"

"I canvassed that diner over there," Murach said, pointing at it. "A waitress there says a guy came in about ten minutes before the shooting started. Says he ordered a sandwich and then got up and left without eating it."

Hall looked sharply at Murach. "Why?"

"She wasn't sure," Murach said with a shrug. "She said he ordered and then when she brought the food he asked for a pay phone and split. Paid for the meal but apparently isn't much of a tipper."

"She give you a description?"

Murach didn't bother referencing his notes. "Big with dark hair. That's about all I got."

"I could have told you that much."

"She was more pissed about the tip than anything else. That's all she really talked about. Just kept *bitching* about the tip."

And now here was Murach bitching about the waitress bitching. "You got her name and address?"

"Yeah."

Hall looked at the body again. "I'll go by later. See if I can get something more out of her. In the meantime, let's get this place cleaned up as quickly as possible."

"What about the shooting team?"

"Screw them assholes," Hall said. "I don't have time for that right now."

BOLAN ENTERED THROUGH the frosted-glass doors of the HIKE squad room at the Phoenix P.D. headquarters on the heels of a uniformed female cop.

A single plainclothes officer occupied one of the many desks within the squad room, and he barely gave them a cursory inspection as they passed before returning his attention to a newspaper. The rest of the room appeared abandoned— quiet as a morgue, almost. The officer led Bolan to an office in back and rapped on the closed door. At the sound of a muffled reply she opened it and poked her head in.

"Someone here to see you, sir," she said.

"Who is it?" the voice asked with an impatient tone.

"Says his name is Cooper. Claims he has information about the shootings today."

"Have him give his statement to Murach."

"Sergeant Murach stepped out, sir," the officer replied with some trepidation.

"Oh, for crissakes, don't—" The man broke off and said, "All right, send him in."

The officer stepped aside and smiled, obviously a bit uncomfortable, and gestured for Bolan to enter.

The Executioner smiled back and nodded as he stepped through the doorway and far enough into the room that the young woman could close the door behind him. The man who stood and came around the desk wasn't anywhere near Bolan's imposing height, maybe five foot ten, and Bolan immediately recognized him as the lead officer he'd shoved out of the way of enemy gunfire earlier that day. Bolan wondered if that man was Captain Joseph Hall, but the letters stenciled on the door of his office had now confirmed it.

The guy reached out a hand and Bolan shook it. Scrutiny, not recognition, flashed in Hall's eyes and Bolan eased out the breath he'd been holding. Hall hadn't gotten a look at his face.

"Have a seat, sir," Hall said.

Bolan casually plopped into the chair as Hall returned to his desk and adjusted his tie. "You have information about what happened today?"

"I was part of what happened today," Bolan replied easily.

Hall's eyes flicked up from his desk and locked on Bolan with a hard stare. Then something dawned on him, something like a realization, and his body tensed.

Bolan held up a palm. "Easy, Hall. I'm not looking for trouble."

"Then you shouldn't have walked in here."

Bolan remained impassive.

Hall continued, "You realize I can arrest you right here just on the *suspicion* that you were involved in today's incident?"

"As long as you realize I'm the one who spared your wife and kids a lot of grief today," Bolan said.

"That's the only reason you're not in handcuffs yet."

"You don't want to do that."

"No. And why not?"

"Let's just say that we're on the same team."

"How do I know that? You a cop?"

"Not exactly."

"Work for the government?"

"Sometimes."

Hall chuckled and sat back in his chair a little, although Bolan noted he still hadn't let down his guard. The Executioner didn't doubt Hall had a gun in reach. "You care to show me some kind of identification to prove that? An authorization signed by the FBI or Justice Department, perhaps?"

Bolan smiled. "Let's pretend for this moment that I'm telling you the truth. Give me five minutes to explain. After that, if you're not convinced, you can do what you like."

"Why should I?"

"The intelligence you got on that meet today was bogus," Bolan said. "The Sinaloa cartel was setting a trap and you walked right into it. If I hadn't intervened when I did, you'd all be dead. That enough reason?"

Hall sat in stony silence for a while before finally saying, "Fine...you got your five minutes."

"Hector Casco wasn't going to be at that meet," Bolan continued. "In fact, I doubt there was any meet at all. I got there before you and I marked five scouts, two above, three at street level."

"It was you at the diner?"

Bolan nodded.

"Yeah, you were a real hit for the waitress there," Hall said matter-of-factly and scratched his neck. He smiled at Bolan and then said, "You care to elaborate on how you know about Hector Casco?"

"I have sources of my own," Bolan said. "I called one of them right before your raid went down. My source told me that this was some of the best hard evidence you'd obtained since the beginning of this year. When I heard that, I figured you'd be itching to jump on it and that you'd do whatever was needed to obtain a warrant. Problem is, Hector Casco had already figured that out."

"So you still haven't answered my question," Hall said. "What do you know about it?"

"A lot. Casco's recent activities here make it obvious he's trying to take over the pipeline from Nogales. Only trouble is, he's playing for keeps, which means he's not looking to take on partners or put up with the competition."

"What's your point, Cooper?"

"That you're about to get in over your head," Bolan said. "Take Ann-Elise McCormack. You think that was about ransom money?"

"Why not?" Hall asked. "What happened this morning. That you, too?"

Bolan nodded. "Montera was already gone when I arrived, but yeah, I'm the one who took down the kidnappers and returned the girl to her home."

"She's one tough kid," Hall replied. "Apparently, every time the FBI asked who it was that rescued her she'd just start crying, insisting she really didn't remember."

"She was grateful," Bolan said. "Look, the fact is that if Casco plans to take control of the drug and gun-running action in this area, things will heat up quickly between him and the competition. Before you know it, you'll have a war on these streets between Los Negros and Los Zetas that'll make what's happening down in Mexico pale by comparison. You've already gotten a taste of how little they care for innocent bystanders."

"So what are you offering?"

"At this point, a sort of partnership," Bolan said. "You can still handle the cases the way you feel you need to, and any intelligence I gather during my own operations, I'll screen and pass on to you if I think it's relevant."

"If it's not enough to get warrants, it does me no good. I got plenty of CI's out there willing to rat out a nickel-and-dime-bag crook for a few bucks. I don't need any more of those."

"It'll be more than enough," Bolan said. "And at least you can rest assured it'll be accurate."

"So you still haven't told me why I should work with you," Hall said. "Or even *trust* you, for that matter. For all I know you could be working for Casco."

"The current case count for your squad is up to what now, Hall, maybe a hundred-sixty?" Bolan calmly asked.

"Something like that, yeah."

"At that rate, I wouldn't be turning down any help."

"But how do I *know* you're legit."

"I could have let you die today," Bolan said and gestured with the flat of his hand. "I could have just walked away and left you and your men to deal on your own."

"What does that prove?"

"Look, Hall, I threw you one lifeline this morning and I'm throwing a second one this evening. The difference is, are you smart enough to reach for it? You're not convinced for the sake of your own life, then at least be convinced for the sake of those you're responsible to protect. There's a war about to break out right here in Phoenix. Maybe I can't stop it, but I might be able to contain it long enough for the spark to die. And I can give you some breathing room to operate so that when you do step in to take down Casco, at least it'll count for something."

Hall fell silent and Bolan gave him the time to let the wheels turn. He could empathize with the policeman but he also didn't have time for games. If Hall didn't go for it, Bolan knew he might end up in a cell. He'd taken a risk doing this, but like most things, the Executioner was playing a hunch and it was one he figured would pay off. Hall and his team had been at it a while and had come up empty-handed, so far. That couldn't be looking good on Hall, a career-minded cop if Bolan didn't miss his guess, and that had to be eating up the guy's insides. Through the years Bolan had become a very good reader of people, and his gut told him Hall would take the deal.

As usual, his gut was right.

"All right, Cooper," Hall said. "We'll try this your way and see where it leads. Where do we start?"

3

The Executioner peered through the night-vision scope of the PSG-1 sniper rifle.

Night had overtaken Phoenix several hours earlier, and Bolan began to feel weariness ebb into his body. In spite of it, his mind remained fully alert to any dangers. There would be plenty of chances to rest later—at least that's what he told himself during the more time-critical missions—but at the moment he needed to stay at peak operational readiness.

The lives of several young women depended on it.

The girls were working in a club owned by Los Negros. When most people heard that name, they typically thought of the Afromestizos group seeking to be recognized as a third ethnic voice within Mexico, a country that had not become a truly pluralist society until the 1990s in order to buy in to the good graces of the United States.

Most didn't know about the *other* Los Negros, a group that had kidnapped, murdered and terrorized the American Southwest. Even with major successes by the DEA and joint agencies in operations like Xcellerator in 2009—the genesis of which began in Imperial County, California, and ultimately spanned more than twenty-five states and seized approximately one billion dollars in Sinaloa cartel assets—the fight continued. Like all such organizations, Los Negros continued to rear its ugly faces like the multiheaded monster it was. Well, Bolan had something for the Hydra, something that it would not soon forget. He had a battle plan, the opening of which involved Bolan behind the sniper rifle, concealed by a tarp over the bed of a large pickup truck. While it might have seemed a crude way of establishing a point from which to strike, it provided Bolan with the position he needed and would buy him the element of surprise. Plus from his vantage point, Bolan had a perfect view of the club entrance.

Initially Hall hadn't been keen on Bolan's plan to turn Los Negros on its ear, but eventually he listened to reason. Bolan convinced him by outlining the wisdom of such a move. There was only one way to keep a guy like Hector Casco from establishing a foothold in Phoenix and that was to turn his operation upside down. And keeping the enemy off balance and teetering on the brink of chaos was what the Executioner did best.

The skintight blacksuit Bolan wore exacerbated the stifling heat. He made a final adjustment to the scope and then pulled his eye away from it long enough to inspect the luminescent hands of his watch. It was nearing 0230 hours and the club had pretty much emptied of the majority of partiers. A few stragglers had emerged in the past thirty minutes—some single men and a few couples, but not Bolan's targets. The warrior realized he could have a very long wait and that wouldn't do, considering the sweat that soaked his body and had on more than one occasion run into his eyes.

The double wooden doors of the club swung outward again, their ornate carvings painted bright hues of red and black, the enamel shimmering under the streetlights. The three VIPs Bolan awaited stepped into the muggy air. All of them were gaudily dressed and accompanied by about a half-dozen bodyguards wearing slacks, silk shirts and black jackets. Each of the VIPs also had a woman on each arm.

At last, Bolan's opportunity had presented itself.

He recognized one of those faces as he lined it up in the blue-green shorthairs of the 6 × 42 scope. A brainchild of Heckler & Koch, the *Präzisionsschorfschützengewehr*-1 sniper rifle dispatched the 7.62 × 51 mm NATO round at a muzzle velocity exceeding 2800 feet per second. With Bolan less than two hundred feet from the guy, he couldn't miss and a first-shot, first-kill probability was imminent.

Even as the first report thundered inside the confines of the truck bed, Bolan had confirmed the hit to the first target and was already working the silent bolt as he swept into acquisition of the next in line. No more than two seconds elapsed before Bolan had taken out the second target with a kill shot that struck the guy in the chest and caused his heart to burst. The bodyguards reacted with incredible enthusiasm—too bad their reactions were so utterly ineffective.

As the bodyguards fanned out and drew their weapons, Bolan was easing back the 3-pound trigger on the third and final target. The round struck the guy in the top of the head and blew his skull and most of his brain out the other side. However, the round struck at just such an angle that the impact sent the hood spinning and he twirled several times with all the grace of a drunken ballerina before collapsing to the pavement.

Bolan withdrew the rifle and pawed at the back of the pickup to lower the tailgate. He coiled his body before launching off the bed and rushing to the driver's side. Bolan hopped into the massive F-350, started the engine and rocketed down the street. He checked his rearview mirror as he did and felt some satisfaction as he saw four of the six gunners rush for a sedan.

Bolan made a hard left at the first street, proceeded two blocks and then made another hard left. He continued on until he passed the first street that would move beyond the club, and then the second, then made one more left. The last thing in the

world the Los Negros thugs would think he would do is return
to the scene. Not to mention they would have their own hands
full in about a minute when a passel of Phoenix P.D. squad
cars suddenly converged on them from every direction.

Bolan rounded the corner and found the two remaining
gunmen seated on the curb, pistols dangling from their hands,
neither of them completely recovered from what had transpired. Bolan bore down on their position and brought the
truck to a screaming halt at the last second so that he was in
a direct line of sight. He aimed out the window with the MP-5
that he'd left on the seat and triggered a sustained burst while
sweeping the muzzle in a rising, corkscrew fashion.

Neither of the Los Negros gunners knew what happened.
The first caught a volley that ripped him open from crotch to
sternum and the second was nearly decapitated by two rounds
that blew his head open. Not to mention the half-dozen or so
rounds that stitched him across the chest.

The quintet of young women were still seated on the sidewalk or hiding behind whatever solid object they'd been able to
find when the shooting started. Bolan collected them quickly
and jabbed a thumb over his shoulder at the truck.

"Get in back," he commanded them.

"No way, mister!" one of the young, frightened girls
screamed and she began to sputter a flurry of curses. "I'm
not going *any*where with *you*."

The others, who had started to comply, now hesitated and
Bolan knew he had to act quickly. He lowered the MP-5 and
raised one hand. "Look, I'm not here to hurt any of you.
I'm here to bring you where it's safe. I'm here to take you
home."

"I ain't got no home!" the girl said in a shaky tone.

"Okay," Bolan said. "Then I'll take you wherever you want
to go, wherever you feel safe. But you can't tell me that's here.
These men have abused you. All of you. And those days are
over for you."

"Oh, yeah?" one of the other girls said. "And what're you expecting in return?"

Bolan kept his voice low. "Nothing. I just want to get you out of here. These are bad men and eventually bad things would have happened to you. I'm giving you a second chance. You can trust me or you can take the risk you'll be right back in a situation like this. Or worse, when their friends come looking for witnesses."

That seemed to convince all but one of them and Bolan made one last, desperate plea, but the girl chose to turn and run. He noted it odd how fast she could run with heels on but then pressed his lips together, shook his head and went to assist the girls into the cab. Once everyone was in, he got behind the wheel and drove away.

"THAT'S YOUR IDEA OF gathering intelligence?"

Bolan shifted the pay-phone receiver to his other ear. "I told you it could get ugly, Hall."

"Is that what you're calling it? Ugly?" Hall sighed. "I've got a whole mess of bodies on my hands and very few answers. I told you before, Cooper, the politicos are breathing down my neck from the special ops chief up to the mayor. You know a representative from the governor's office showed up here this morning, for crissakes? I thought we had an agreement."

"We did," Bolan replied. "And I'm sticking to it."

"How so?"

"I noticed you mentioned the dead bodies but not the four live ones sitting in your jail cell."

"You mean those four who lawyered up? What good are they going to be?"

Bolan clucked his tongue. "I can't control what happens inside your house, Hall. So far I've delivered just what I promised—don't try to back out."

For a long time Hall didn't say anything to that. Bolan hated having to bottom-line the cop but he didn't have time for games. The fact remained he'd held up his end of the bargain and he was going to need Hall's support.

"You realize what you're asking me to do? You want me to look the other way while you start a war right here."

"I'm trying to prevent a war, not start one," Bolan reminded him. "The Los Negros aren't going to just roll over any more than Los Zetas did in Nuevo Laredo. And you can bet Hector Casco's burning up the phone lines right now trying to figure out what happened. That kind of traffic is sure to give you more leads. I know you have at least a few of their operating locations under surveillance."

Hall chuckled. "Well I'll be…"

"What?"

"I'd sure like to know where you get your information," Hall said. "You obviously knew almost as much about our ops as I did. And you're such an enigmatic bastard you don't have any record. It's like you don't exist, Cooper. No fingerprints, no driver's license and no financial records."

"You checked on me."

"Can you blame me?"

"No, I would have done the same."

"So what do you have up your sleeve next? Run a tank through the Sinaloa cartel's headquarters?"

"Nothing quite so dramatic," Bolan replied. "As I said, I figure Casco will be making inquiries and he'll probably be working up some sort of retaliation."

"You want him to assume that Los Zetas did the hit."

"Exactly. That's why I took the girls off the streets, too."

"What about the one that got away?"

"I'm hoping she'll go underground," Bolan said as a grim lump formed in his gut.

"If she tries to contact others inside Los Negros and gives up what actually happened, your plan might fall apart."

"If she contacts them she'll only end up dead, which unfortunately could be the very best to hope for. Casco won't take this lying down. I believe he'll respond and he'll do it quickly. He can't afford not to."

"And how's that going to help us?" Hall asked.

"Wherever Casco hits Los Zetas, he's going to make noise doing it. That's going to draw attention and when it goes down I'm going to be one of the first to hear about it."

"How do you know that?"

"I can't tell you that," Bolan said.

The tone in Hall's voice betrayed he wasn't happy with Bolan's response. "A relationship like ours is built on trust, Cooper. We got nothing else going for us."

"I can't tell you, so let's leave it alone. What I can tell you is that when I do hear about Casco's retaliation, it will come from the same place I heard your men were walking into a trap at that raid."

"Well, that particular bit of information saved my life and those of about six good men. I guess it'll have to be enough— but only for now."

"I understand the position you're in, Hall. I have a suggestion for you if you'd like to hear it."

"Shoot."

"Call the Department of Justice in Washington. Ask to talk to a guy named Brognola. Just explain your situation and ask him what he might be able to do to get some of the heat off your back. I can promise your troubles will abate by sundown."

"Brognola, huh?"

"Yeah."

Hall sighed again. "Okay, I'll give that a shot."

"As soon as I have something for you, I'll call back."

Bolan disconnected the call, field-stripped his cigarette and returned to his car. He couldn't have risked making that call on his phone. The warrior didn't doubt for a moment that one or more of Casco's people monitored the airways. The Los Negros network was larger and more powerful than even Joseph Hall would have admitted, and Bolan couldn't see risking his demise over sloppy tactics. Such decisions had saved his life many times before.

As he got behind the wheel, Bolan's cell phone vibrated, demanding attention. He saw the number, recognized it and answered. "Yeah, it's me."

"Can you meet me?" Vince Gagliardi's voice inquired.

"Where and when?"

"I'll get back to you within an hour."

Dead air followed and Bolan realized Gagliardi had hung up. He pushed the disconnect button, stared a moment at the screen and then tucked the phone in his shirt pocket. The call had all of Bolan's senses on alert. The Executioner and Gagliardi had agreed that if the DEA agent sensed he might be in trouble or his cover blown, he'd contact Bolan with those words so that Bolan would know to stay clear. Their agreement was if something like that went down, no calls and no meetings.

Okay, so the heat was already ramping up. Bolan had figured that his assault on Casco's three underbosses at the club might generate quite a bit of suspicion. After all, the police wouldn't have conducted such an attack, which narrowed the possible source of information regarding Los Negros's use of the club as an official meeting place for Casco's people. That left either the hitters coming from Los Zetas or a traitor inside Los Negros. The search for a leak would eventually work its way into Los Zetas, as well, and that would put Gagliardi at risk irrespective of the fact he was still pretty low in the ranks.

Bolan had prepared for such an eventuality. He knew he'd have to tap some alternate sources of information. His first concern had to be Gagliardi, however. He didn't want to blow the DEA agent's cover but he also owed the guy a hell of a lot. He couldn't just take the risk that Gagliardi would be discovered, never mind the fact that if Gagliardi got blown,

Casco's people would force him to talk. The DEA trained their undercover agents to resist many forms of torture, but *every* man had a breaking point: Gagliardi couldn't hold out forever.

Bolan keyed in a number by heart and the voice of Aaron Kurtzman answered on the first ring. Affectionately known as "Bear" among his close friends and allies, Kurtzman served as Stony Man's chief technical wizard. He was a specialist at computer programs, data manipulation and retrieval and cybersecurity; he commanded a team of some of the greatest technical minds ever assembled. The skills of his team rivaled even those in places like NASA, DARPA and the NSA.

"Striker, how are you?" Kurtzman greeted his friend.

"Doing good, Bear." Bolan hadn't planned to enlist his Stony Man friends but with the life of a DEA agent and good man on the line, he didn't see much choice. "I need your help."

"Name it."

"I need to get a location on a DEA agent named Gagliardi, first name of Vincent. He's currently working an undercover narco op here in Phoenix. His probable location should be recorded in the files of his case officer."

"And you need me to crack it."

"You mind?"

Kurtzman let out a booming laugh. "You kidding? Been looking for a little excitement since I got back from leave. How soon you need it?"

"Yesterday," Bolan replied. "This guy's in trouble, and I need to find him before his cover's blown."

"Give me a quarter-hour and I'll call you back."

"Roger that. And thanks, Bear."

"Don't mention it."

True to his word, Kurtzman called fifteen minutes later with a location. Bolan hadn't even bothered changing out of his blacksuit. He barely had time to return to his hotel and retrieve his equipment bag, where his full arsenal was stowed. There might not be another chance. The mission had gone into high gear. The stakes were up and the numbers were running down. A totality of the circumstances had dictated the parameters of the mission this time, and Bolan found little choice but to follow the trail Fate had laid ahead of him. Either way, it didn't matter to Bolan. If he could create more chaos for Casco by hitting Los Zetas while buying Gagliardi time to break away from whatever mess he'd stepped in, so much the better.

Bolan had become an expert in improvisation long ago. From jungle hell-grounds to battlefields littered with *Mafioso* vermin, the Executioner forged a new kind of warfare. He'd learned to hit the enemy hard and fast, give them no corner. He continued his War Everlasting with the maintenance of one primal goal: put the enemy down and keep them there. And that's what Bolan had come to Phoenix to do.

Yeah, the Sun City blitz had begun.

4

"I'm telling you, Rumaldo, this *cabrón* was no damned Zeta. This dude was some kind of soldier or something."

Rumaldo Salto, enforcer and head of Hector Casco's personal guard, folded his meaty arms and leaned against a pillar of the portico outside Casco's home. "A soldier, eh?"

"Yeah," Claudia Pacorbo said. "Like a commando, see. Dressed all in black. Big and mean. And he had some kind of special gun, you know, like an automatic gun."

The story was too wild to make up and yet Salto had serious trouble believing her. For one thing, Pacorbo was known to do a little too much nose candy and that kind of habit didn't promote clear thinking. Second, the boss had assigned him to stay put and watch the house and grounds while he sent his spies to the streets to get the full story. But nearly an hour before dawn, Pacorbo showed up at the front gate in a taxi cab without a dime to her name—Salto had to fork out nearly a hundred bucks for Pacorbo's twenty-mile ride from south-central Phoenix to the east side of Scottsdale—with a cockamamie story about a commando dressed all in black and toting a machine gun.

Then again, Salto had already heard the first reports coming back as evidence that supported Pacorbo's wild story. First, two of the guys assigned to protect Casco's chief shot-callers were dead and riddled with too many bullets to have come from one or two guns. Second, the other girls had gotten into the truck this alleged commando had been driving under the promise he was going to "take them home." *That* most definitely smelled of serious trouble. The only thing Salto wondered was if the trouble was coming from the cops, Los Zetas, or a freelance troublemaker looking to score some action.

"Okay…okay, *chica*. I'll tell you what, I'll talk to the boss and see if he'll meet with you. But I'm telling you, girl, if you're pulling my leg just to score some money for smack, you're going to *get* a smack. And it won't be the kind you're thinking."

"Fine," Pacorbo said, tossing her dark hair over her shoulder with smug indifference. She folded her arms and added, "You go talk to Hector."

Salto shot her a dirty look before turning to head inside. The cool air felt good against his face. Barely morning out there and it was already muggy and hot. Salto wasn't much for the heat, a surprising twist of fate for a native-born Mexican raised near Juárez on the American-Mexican border. Before joining Los Negros, Salto had trained quite a while in the Sonoran Desert and resided for some time in Hermosillo. Eventually, like so many of his Los Negros brothers, Salto entered the U.S. illegally for the sole purpose of working in the employ of Hector Casco.

The honor was all Salto's, no doubts there. Casco turned out to be one who ruled with a firm but fair hand, and while he didn't pay that well, he treated each man with dignity. In fact, most wouldn't have looked at a guy like Casco and marked him as the second ranking overseer of the Sinaloa cartel. Casco was known among certain circles as a man of distinct tastes who prepossessed a classic air of style and dignity. Additionally, Casco donated to a number of worthwhile charities—anonymously, of course, since it wouldn't do for his enemies to know his true identity—while rubbing elbows with the social elite in Scottsdale under an assumed identity.

It was Casco's ability to continue his charade of identity that amazed Salto most. The fact nobody had yet betrayed him spoke to his skill in this area. Actually no one, with the exception of the heads of the Sinaloa cartel, even knew the details of Casco's alternate alias. They were not allowed to accompany him to the various social events in which he engaged, save for his driver, And neither Salto nor any of the house protection team were permitted to leave the grounds except when off duty.

Salto had once considered following Casco but decided against it as too risky. If he were discovered they would most certainly mark him as a cop or a traitor, and a traitor's mark was not something he wanted to acquire while inside Los Negros. Not only could it mean death, but even if he were to explain it as mere curiosity he would also be ostracized and no longer enjoy the freedoms and protection of the organization. Salto had worked too hard, come too far, to *ever* let that happen.

Salto rapped on the slightly ajar door to Casco's study, and then poked his head through the opening at a grunt of acknowledgement. Casco sat at his desk scribbling furiously on a notepad. There wasn't a phone or computer in sight; Casco didn't believe in such things as they could be traced back to him. There was a house phone but that was all. Any correspondence was either handwritten, output via a thermal typewriter or delivered in-person between Casco's couriers.

A courier had been Salto's first job after coming into Casco's employ. The job was tough and extremely dangerous given the list of Casco's innumerable enemies. A courier was nothing more than an information mule. He carried nothing of material value, but the knowledge a courier possessed was priceless to rival gangs, and particularly to Los Zetas. None of Casco's enemies had ever caught a courier, which is probably why Casco continued to operate with the freedom he did. Still, he knew that luck wouldn't last forever. Eventually, they'd get to a courier and the guy would spill his guts, and then Salto would have to start earning his money for real.

"What is it, Maldo?" Casco demanded, using a shortened form of Salto's name. Nobody else but Hector called him that.

"Boss, the Pacorbo chick demands to see you."

"I'm busy," Casco snapped. "And I'm not about to give that bitch any more money. You tell her to go suck it off Julio or one of the clubbers. She ain't going to get change from me. I know what a gold-hopping whore she is."

"Uh, sure, boss…but—"

Casco had returned to his work as if he hadn't heard Salto. Nearly a full minute passed before he looked up and noticed his house boss still standing there and pinned him with an icy stare.

Salto took a deep breath and blurted it out before he got in trouble. "She showed up here looking pretty hard, Hector. And she claims that what happened to our boys last night was not the doing of Los Zetas."

"Bullshit."

"That's what I told her and she insisted."

"And you believed her?"

"When she tells me to basically go fuck myself if I don't let me see you, yeah, that gets me to start wondering. And then she tells me about this dude, the guy that she claims took them out, dressed all in black like some kind of commando, shooting this chatter gun and stuff. And she claims he took out all three of our guys from quite a distance, almost like a sniper or something."

Casco's pallor went a noticeable gray, and something flickered in his eyes. "Did you say he was dressed all in black?"

When Salto nodded, Casco's mouth dropped open as if he wanted to say something.

"What is it, boss?"

"If that's true, then that is a problem…a very serious fucking problem."

It wasn't often that Casco got excitable, but Salto could tell this had his boss on edge. He talked as if his mouth was dry as cotton, and some beads of sweat were visible as they glimmered in the light. Casco had a reputation of being a tough, fearless son of a bitch who didn't worry about nothing or nobody. Yet every day the guy had to worry his enemies would track him down and kill him. He had to worry about underlings who might betray him, and rivals who might try to undercut his operations.

"You know who this guy is?"

"Maybe," Casco said, clearing his throat. "Maybe I do. You remember Jose Carillo?"

"Panchos Carillo?"

When Casco slowly nodded, Salto felt a stabbing sensation to his chest. The very name conjured a cornucopia of memories. Most of it had been before Salto's time, but he couldn't imagine too many guys his age not hearing the legend of Jose "Panchos" Carillo. The deceased Mexican mob leader had brokered a deal with the Revolutionary Armed Forces of Columbia to provide protection for his massive drug-smuggling operations after the collapse of his only rival's empire. Unfortunately, an equally determined faction of a Chinese triad known as the Kung Lok had set their sights on the American Southwest, as well.

As the story went, one man was credited with bringing down both sides in a bloodbath that lasted a couple of weeks and went from Las Vegas, Los Angeles and El Paso to Canada. It was even rumored that this same bastard—who dressed in black and used military tactics—took the fight to Hong Kong and closed the attempted Kung Lok operation into utter chaos. Carillo and his closest advisors were eliminated, along with some high-ranking officials in the American government, and this individual was credited with racking up a body count so great on both sides that they never recovered.

"You don't think—"

Casco lifted a hand to cut him off. "We won't make any assumptions. The first thing we must do is verify this. Go get the bitch."

Salto turned and immediately retrieved Pacorbo. As they entered Casco's study, Salto caught the strong odor of cigar smoke. This surprised him, since his boss didn't typically smoke in his home. He chose to go outside to enjoy his cigars, and the fact he'd fired up inside the house—in his study, no less—told Salto all he needed to know about how his boss was taking this news.

"Have a seat," he said to Pacorbo, gesturing to a nearby couch.

She practically fell into the plush cushions and propped her feet on the coffee table in a most disrespectful fashion. Salto looked in Casco's direction with horror but it seemed his boss decided to overlook the indiscretion. He would have ordered the bottoms of the feet beaten of anyone else who had done such a thing. Casco appreciated fine furniture and didn't tolerate anyone treating his possessions with indifference.

Casco sat on the edge of his desk and took a long mouthful of smoke, letting it out slowly before he addressed Pacorbo. "Maldo tells me you have some information about the man who killed three of my people last night."

Pacorbo said, "You damn bet I do. But I got a question for you, first."

Casco smiled but it lacked graciousness. "And what might that be?"

"What would this information be worth to you?" Pacorbo said. "Because once I tell you what I saw, I'm gonna have to get out of here for a while. Lay low."

"Why's that?" Salto asked.

"Quiet," Casco said to him. He returned his attention to

Pacorbo. "I would have to give the matter some additional consideration, but I suppose that I would initially ask you the same question."

Pacorbo expressed confusion. "Say what?"

"How much is the information worth to *you?* Is it worth say, perhaps…your life? Or maybe it is not so much, maybe it is only worth one or two of your fingers. Or how about a nipple? After all, you have two of them."

"What're you talking about? You know me, Hector."

"Yes, I do." Casco took another purposeful draw from the cigar before continuing. "Which is what begs the question, does it not? You are known for being an opportunist, Claudia, and loose enough to do anything for a little blow. You are also a noted loudmouth, and obnoxious with a zest that borders on stupidity. How you ever got the nickname of Angel I will never understand, because you are anything but. So here is my proposal. If what you tell me sounds legitimate, I will allow you to leave here with all of your body parts intact. I will even arrange for a one-way trip to anywhere you wish. If you lie to me, however, or I believe you are exaggerating even a little, I will have to reconsider our relationship and refer you to some people who are not reputed to be lenient toward your kind."

Pacorbo sat in stunned silence.

Salto had to admit that Casco's words had surprised him a bit, as well. He'd never seen Casco lose his temper beyond a show of irritability here and there, and he certainly hadn't heard the guy make open threats. On some level, Salto marked Casco's reputation as a very dangerous man. Salto had already believed it, for the most part, but this exchange only served to reinforce any doubts that might have crept into his mind.

"So would you like to proceed telling me exactly what you saw or have you changed your mind?"

"I saw what I saw, Hector. I don't give a shit if you believe me or not, but I saw what I saw."

"Okay, then, I'm listening."

Pacorbo took a deep breath and then burst into a five-minute dissertation on everything she had seen and heard, leaving out none of even the smallest details. Salto would intermittently look at the boss's face, but Casco sat in such stony silence that Salto couldn't get a read on how her words affected him up or down. When Pacorbo finished her spiel, Casco took several thoughtful minutes to consider what she had said, puffing absently at his cigar. Finally, he mashed the stogie into a giant glass ashtray on his desk, folded his arms and stared at Pacorbo.

"You know something, Angel...I believe you. I really believe you."

Salto produced a deep sigh of relief under his breath at the same time as Pacorbo produced an audible one, and Salto realized both of them had been on pins and needles. That's when Casco's next statement caught him totally off guard.

"Maldo, take her out of here. Make sure she doesn't come back."

"What?" Pacorbo screamed.

Pacorbo started to stand but the deep cushions made it difficult, and before she could gain her feet, Casco stepped forward and slapped her hard across the side of the head. The blow sent the young woman reeling. She landed against the sharp edge of the marble coffee table, the blow enough to split open the skin on her scalp but not render her completely unconscious. Pacorbo let out a shrill cry and tried to stand, but before Salto could react, Casco was all over her.

"Boss, what are you—?"

"Shut up!"

Casco turned furiously onto the woman and began to pummel her with his fists. A couple of times he kicked her in the tailbone with the heel of his shoe, a move that made Salto wince a bit. Salto stood almost twice the size of Casco, and yet he remained still and rigid as if his legs were cemented into the floor. After at least a full two minutes of continuous brutality, Casco ceased the battering and straightened his shirt collar. All that remained of Pacorbo was a whimpering, sobbing mass of bruised flesh.

Casco looked at Salto and his expression left no doubt as to the intent behind his words. "Get her out of here."

Casco was ordering Salto to take Pacorbo from there and dispose of her—but why? It had been some time since Salto had to bust a cap on anyone, and he couldn't ever remember doing a woman. Not a helpless, defenseless woman like Pacorbo. What threat could she truly pose to him?

Well, it didn't matter much because Salto knew damn good and well if he didn't do as he was told that he'd be the one Casco ordered eliminated. And that just wouldn't do. Reluctantly, but with haste so as not to incur further wrath, Salto dragged the poor, battered woman to her feet and hauled her ass out of there. She moaned and her head lolled on her chest, but she was only semiconscious. As he half dragged, half carried her limp form across the tile floors of the hallway to the front foyer—her stiletto heels click-clacking with eerie regularity whenever they hit the seams between the tiles—Salto noticed no blood other than from her scalp wound.

So Hector hadn't hit her in the face or any areas that would draw blood. He'd struck her only with body blows. Why? Was it something about disfiguring a woman that maybe bothered Casco? If he had, it certainly would have bothered Salto. He wasn't into beating on women, as a general rule, much less offing them. But if Hector said it had to be done, it had to be done.

Salto got her into one of the house cars, a plain sedan, and clubbed her with the butt of his pistol. He thought about putting her in the backseat but then thought better of it and opted for the trunk.

The drive down to a secluded area of the city beneath the I-10 freeway took ten minutes. He hauled her from the trunk and dumped her onto the cement. Salto pulled his pistol and put it close to her head. He took a deep breath, willing himself to get it over with, but his hand began to shake. What the hell was *wrong* with him? He'd done this shit so many times he couldn't remember the count. Yet here he was like a scared little girl, not even able to end this little tramp's misery. Maybe that was because deep down he actually liked Claudia Pacorbo a bit.

After another minute of indecision, Salto stowed his pistol. He pulled a roll of cash from his pocket and peeled off a few hundred bucks. He then scrawled out a quick note that read, "Leave and don't ever come back." He stuffed the cash and note in an exposed portion of her bra.

Then Salto jumped into his car and drove away, never looking back.

5

Bolan approached the large auto-repair garage in what Gagliardi had called one of the harshest and grittiest commercial zones in Phoenix. Across a parking lot of more rubble than concrete was a convenience store. On the other side was an abandoned business building with all of the windows smashed, leaving only metal bars to deter burglars, vagrants and any other riffraff from entering the building.

The Executioner wasn't reticent in the actions he was about to undertake. While he'd agreed on how to play this with Gagliardi, the situation had changed some and Bolan felt justified. Gagliardi had risked his life and nearly flushed eighteen months of undercover work down the toilet just to get intelligence to Bolan for the sake of camaraderie. Bolan didn't see it as an option to casually walk away from the situation when things went hard.

One way or another, he planned to snatch Gagliardi out of trouble before the man lost his life—damn the consequences. He'd face the challenge of taking down Los Zetas once he knew Gagliardi was safe.

Bolan cruised past the garage's blackened windows. He noted that one of the three large metal doors was partially open. A figure lay on a creeper beneath a late-model Chevy, working diligently at the undercarriage. Or at least that's how he wanted it to appear. Loud vocals in Spanish accompanied by what sounded like Latin rhythms and music poured from the garage, echoing through the early morning air.

Bolan shook his head as he took in the sight and then continued down the block. He checked his watch: barely a quarter past 0700 hours. It was *much* too early for a legitimate garage to be open with men already at work. The Executioner knew exactly what he was dealing with. The mechanic was actually a sentry, and he was betting a whole mess of Los Zetas hardcases were encamped within the building. He was also betting that Gagliardi was among them, and that the Zetas might even be subjecting him to "interrogation" at that very moment.

SPECIAL AGENT Vincent Gagliardi braced himself for what he knew was coming.

Another teeth-jarring punch connected with his face. His head reeled and Gagliardi could almost sense the neurons dying as his brain bounced around inside his skull. He'd nearly made it out of the garage but two of the biggest members of Los Zetas managed to grab him as he was cutting out, just moments after warning off Cooper. They stripped him down to underwear, tied him to a chair and blindfolded him. After smoking and joking amongst each other for nearly a half hour, already drinking tequila and bolstering their courage for the task ahead, the abuses began.

What Gagliardi couldn't figure out was how they'd made him. He'd been careful, *very* careful, during his meetings with Cooper. He'd also regularly swept his run-down studio in the projects for bugs, scanned his cell phone and regularly shredded or burned anything that might connect him with the DEA. He made sure whenever muling that he didn't talk to any members outside of Los Zetas, and he only funneled reports once a month to his supervisor by a secure, electronic transmission from a safe house. Yet somehow, despite being careful, he'd tripped up somewhere and they'd found out he wasn't one of them.

They wanted to know who he worked for, and Gagliardi knew that he'd only be able to hold out so long. At the moment, though, they weren't even asking him questions. They simply continued beating on him, holding smoldering cigarettes close to the tender flesh on his inner thighs. Gagliardi tried to block it out, to think of his beloved Natalie and their precious little Samantha, but not agonize over the possibility that they might grow old without him. Natalie had begged him not to take this assignment, citing a dozen reasons why she had a bad feeling about it.

Gagliardi had learned to listen to those premonitions over the years, but he'd been blinded by a move that would solidify his career in the DEA. If he pulled off this stint, pulled it off successfully, he knew he could look forward to many years behind a desk as a handler or even a supervising agent.

Of course, it had looked really good at the time they offered it to him. Now he didn't know whether any of it would pan out. Probably not. They would beat him senseless, use him up; they might not ask any questions at all, or they would save the questions for later. Much later. After they had beaten and humiliated him until they were satiated. Los Zetas would make an example of him, almost certainly.

There wouldn't be any saving avenger this time. Gagliardi had waved off the only guy who could possibly help him, so now he was on his own.

Yeah, things looked pretty grim indeed.

He would miss his family desperately.

BOLAN CUT A HARD LEFT and parked in the lot of a grocery store that hadn't opened yet. There were a few cars in the lot, probably opening staff, so at least his vehicle wouldn't look completely out of place. Bolan retrieved his arsenal bag from the trunk and hoofed it across the street and down an alley that he had spotted on his reconnoiter. He'd have to go in soft, make sure he could locate Gagliardi and scope out the odds. No point hitting the place with guns blazing only to get both himself and the DEA agent killed in the process.

Bolan stopped short of the alleyway where it emerged onto the street near the garage and crouched in the shadows.

The Beretta 93-R, cleaned and ready for action, already rode in shoulder leather. Bolan withdrew the MP-5SD3, a retractable butt variant featuring sound-suppression and 3-shot-burst capability, and checked the action. He slung the weapon and then withdrew the military web belt sporting the holstered .44 Magnum Desert Eagle and clipped it around his waist. He stood now in blacksuit, weapons of war dangling from his body, and looked every bit as formidable as the legend that preceded him.

Bolan secured the bag that collapsed into a butt pack when lightened of its load. He then left the alley and dashed across the street, diligent to stay out of view of the guard under the car. He pressed his back to the wall of the garage when he'd reached the other side and edged toward the mouth of the open bay. Bolan risked a glance around the corner, spotted the exposed legs of the sentry and then slipped quietly inside and grabbed the man's pant leg.

Bolan yanked hard and the creeper slid obediently on the cement, bringing the sentry full into Bolan's view. The soldier promptly clamped a hand over the man's mouth, dropped his full weight onto his abdomen with a knee and pinned him with an icy gaze. It took Bolan only a millisecond to realize, though, that this "man" was really little more than a boy, maybe sixteen or seventeen.

Bolan eased the muzzle of the MP-5SD3 into view to give the kid a good, long look. He whispered, "Cry out or make a sound, you're dead. Understand?"

The kid nodded very slowly, the fear evident that he understood Bolan perfectly.

"How many are inside?" Bolan asked as he removed his hand.

"Me…mebbe five?" the kid stammered in a heavy Spanish accent.

"You don't sound sure."

The youth nodded. "Five. Yes, there's five…no wait!"

"Shh!" Bolan ordered.

The kid realized he'd been talking too loudly. It was unlikely anybody could hear them over the music blaring from a stereo system in the nearby office—Bolan could barely hear himself think it was so loud—but better not to take any chances.

"There is one dude, not us."

Bolan didn't understand at first, given the kid's broken English, but then he realized that the kid most likely meant Gagliardi, and that they had discovered he wasn't one of the them. The Los Zetas and Los Negros were notorious for atrocities when they discovered outsiders among their ranks. That was one of the reasons it had been difficult for agents even of the Mexican government to get inside these gangs. It was a closed circle, requiring an almost bloody initiation ceremony, the rites of passage typically included committing either a rape, kidnapping, murder or all of the above.

Bolan felt a bit of empathy for kids this age who were drawn into the lifestyle. He probably worked on the gang's cars, maybe even apprenticed with a relative to take his place since most initiated members of such groups weren't typically long for the world. That's what most people didn't understand. This way of life was very much like living in a war-torn country. These young men, boys really, had to watch each other's backs so they didn't get a bullet or shank in them. They were prisoners of a sort of perverse society that thrived on mayhem and crime, the vices of others. Every dime of money, or at least a large chunk of it, that went into the hands of drug dealers in America eventually ended up back in the coffers of criminal enterprises just like these.

That's what supported the life. Well, Bolan had it in mind to place embargoes on this particular trade and so far he was doing a pretty good job of it, if it could be measured in effective results. He had eliminated three of Hector Casco's high-ranking members, and he was just about to put a dent in the number of Casco's enemies. To Bolan's way of thinking, it was really rather profound.

"Where are they?" Bolan asked.

The kid gestured toward the back of the garage.

Bolan nodded, stood, grabbed a fistful of the kid's dirty T-shirt and hauled him to his feet.

Bolan stood to height and looked down at the teenager, who had to be a full six inches shorter. "You've picked the wrong side, young man. Leave here and find some place to make a better life for yourself. Find a shelter and get help. And don't ever come back here, because there won't be anything to come back to. Understand?"

The kid nodded and then Bolan jerked his head and the youth sprinted from the garage without so much as a word or backward glance.

When he'd disappeared, Bolan whirled on his heel and proceeded in the direction the kid had indicated. He eventually found a metal door that led down a narrow hallway. The corridor opened onto another room and amidst a dimly lit, smoke-filled room there were five men cloistered around Gagliardi. They were all laughing and smoking, passing a tequila bottle and playing what looked to be some kind of game that involved taking a deep hit off a marijuana joint, pounding several hard swallows of tequila and then hauling off with a punch to Gagliardi's face.

The DEA agent sat in the middle of the room wearing only briefs, his legs spread, and bound to a rickety chair that threatened to break under him with every punch. Bolan couldn't see his face that well, most of it obscured by a blindfold that looked like it was made from a ratty T-shirt. Bolan took the sight in quickly and pressed his lips together as he considered his options. There were no lights in the hallway, so the deep shadows concealed his black-clad form.

Opening up with his SMG in those confines wasn't practical; he risked hitting Gagliardi no matter how good a marksman he was. Taking them out with a pistol might have been viable but he couldn't be sure to get all five of the men before one of them did Gagliardi. Wading among them with bare hands was suicide, obviously—unless he could find a way to distract them.

Decided on the best tactic, Bolan reached into a concealed pocket of his blacksuit and withdrew a pair of gray-colored grenades with red bands across their centers. The ABC-M25A2 riot control grenades contained a CS1 filler mixed with silica aerogel for increased efficiency of gas disbursement. The CS gas was military-grade designed for riot control, making it about three times stronger than that used by law enforcement. This particular version had been modified by Stony Man's chief weaponsmith, John "Cowboy" Kissinger, to blow with the same effect as a flashbang.

Bolan pulled the pins and tossed them into the corners of the room farthest from any windows so that the bits of shrapnel didn't accidentally hit Gagliardi and the smoke wasn't vented out. He then crouched, opened his mouth, closed his eyes and clapped his hands over his ears. The tinkling of metal striking cement drew the attention of the drug- and alcohol-dazed men, but they took no notice of Bolan.

The concussion hit the room suddenly, and the flash temporarily blinded all five thugs. The gas burst from the grenades with tremendous force, aided by the silica aerogel, and Bolan immediately whipped the portable goggles and ten-minute mask from the butt pack and donned it expertly. Bolan cut through the smoke, rocketing a palm into the mastoid process behind the ear of one dazed gang member to clear the path to Gagliardi. The others were choking, their lungs and eyes no doubt rendered with the sensations of being on fire.

Bolan shouted a consolation to Gagliardi as he whipped a KA-BAR knife into play and cut the man's bonds. He hauled Gagliardi onto his shoulder and beat a hasty exit from the noxious environment. He was sorry for his prize having to go through such a traumatic experience after getting his brains beat in, but Gagliardi hadn't been exposed to anything from which he wouldn't physically recover. The emotional and psychological scars would probably last much longer, irrespective of any training Gagliardi might have undergone before taking the assignment.

Once Bolan had him well clear of the scene, he put Gagliardi down long enough to rip the chemical mask from his face and stow it. He then brought the MP-5SD3 into battery, got Gagliardi on his feet and pulled the blindfold from the man's eyes. Gagliardi blinked a few times, shook his head and had to look at Bolan for a time before he recognized him.

"Am I glad to see you," Gagliardi said with a grin.

"Likewise," Bolan said.

Some of the gas had dispelled and come down the hallway, and the clang of the door opening signaled the enemy was hot on their trail. Bolan drew his Beretta, grabbed Gagliardi's hand and shoved the pistol into it. "Time to go. Can you make it on your own?"

"You kidding?" Gagliardi said.

"Then let's move out."

The two men burst from the garage, Gagliardi taking the lead as Bolan gestured in the direction of the alleyway before turning and running backward to provide rear cover. They were nearly across the street when two of the posse emerged from the bay door and looked wildly around, ugly machine pistols clutched in their fists. They spotted Bolan and Gagliardi simultaneously and raised the muzzles in their direction.

Bolan continued moving backward, glancing only occasionally to ensure a clear path as he tracked the enemy with his MP-5SD3 and opened up full-auto burn. The move was meant more to keep heads down and dissuade pursuit than engage a target, but Bolan's efficiency as a marksman rewarded him with a prize. The sustained volley caught one of the hardcases across the midsection and he dropped to the pavement with a shredded belly full of 9 mm Parabellum slugs.

His partner realized the enemy wasn't so helpless and left off returning fire in a moment of self-preservation. Bolan took the guy before he could find cover, blowing off the top of his head with a short burst. A second burst caught the gunner in the left shoulder and spun him on impact. He bounced off a telephone pole and pitched forward to land hard on the concrete.

A squeal of tires drew Bolan's attention and he spotted a dark Chevy round a corner a half-block down from their position. The Executioner sent another furious stream of lead at the remaining trio of Los Zetas, who appeared at the fringes of the open bay before turning and sprinting after Gagliardi. The situation had suddenly gone hard, and Bolan had to wonder for a moment if he'd slipped up somewhere and exposed himself to Los Zetas informants.

Either way, if they died here it wouldn't make a whole lot of difference. This wasn't the ideal place to make their stand anyway, especially not on foot against a numerically superior force. The pair continued down the alleyway, reaching the next block just as the Chevy turned in to it at the other end and accelerated with the roar of its powerful engine.

Gagliardi paused a moment, chest heaving, and looked helplessly at Bolan. The warrior waved him on, indicating he should continue in any direction but that of the approaching vehicle. The Executioner's legs pumped him along, muscles fed by blood and adrenaline aching with the strain. The combat stretch felt good, but Bolan didn't much like being exposed to the enemy in this fashion. If he didn't come up with a retaliatory plan soon, or at least a decent tactical retreat, both he and Gagliardi were dead.

Bolan reached the mouth of the alley and dove to his right a heartbeat before the Chevy ran him down. The vehicle jounced onto the street and the driver had to jam on the brakes and perform some pretty fancy moves to keep control of the top-heavy vehicle. Unfortunately for him, he wasn't as good as he thought he was. The Chevy lurched with the strain, skidded sideways until it reached the sidewalk and then flipped onto its side and tipped precariously, rocking a bit before finally landing on the roof.

Bolan climbed to his feet, nodded at the favored hand that had been dealt them and then pressed toward the vehicle. Gagliardi had apparently noted Bolan's ride at their last meeting because he found the DEA agent waiting, sweeping the muzzle of his pistol in every direction to cover Bolan's approach.

The Executioner ripped the butt pack from his waist and tossed it to Gagliardi, then both men hopped into the waiting sedan. Bolan fired the engine to life and cut away from the scene as if the Hounds of Hell were on their tail. They merged onto the street and as they left the area, Gagliardi looked behind them. "Shit! More company!"

6

Bolan's eyes flicked toward the mirror.

This vehicle was silver, the lines of a BMW or Mercedes, but at that distance it was difficult to be certain. Bolan regretted his position behind the wheel, wishing just for a moment he'd let Gagliardi drive. Well, there wasn't much he could do about it now. Bolan reached into his pocket and withdrew his cell phone, then handed it to Gagliardi.

"What? What do you want me to do with this?"

"Call your handler, let him know what's going on," Bolan said. "Tell him you've been blown and we're hot. Tell him to call Captain Joseph Hall and let him know our situation."

"You crazy?" Gagliardi expressed incredulity. "What are they going to be able to do for us?"

"Nothing," Bolan said. "But I have the feeling this is about to get ugly and I want them to clear as many bystanders out of the way as possible."

"Okay, but I still don't get it."

Bolan sighed, not accustomed to explaining himself. He operated with professional combatants most of the time, when he wasn't operating alone, and those combatants typically followed his orders to the letter without question or argument. Gagliardi came from a different background and wasn't used to just following anyone so blindly. In fact, while he'd been undercover the past sixteen months, he called all the shots with little to no outside interference.

Bolan replied, "Los Zetas aren't going to give us up easily, especially since they think we're working for Los Negros."

"Why would they think that?"

"There's been a war brewing between these factions for a while, Vince," Bolan said. "Surely you've seen that much."

"What did you do?" Gagliardi asked. "You *did* something, didn't you, Cooper?"

"You know Casco's three lieutenants who went down in front of their club?"

"The hit last night," Gagliardi said, a dawn of realization spreading across his features. *"You?"*

Bolan nodded. "Yeah, and I'm sorry about that. It's probably what got you burned."

"But how would they have ever tied that to me?"

"Nothing saying they did," Bolan replied.

"But you just said—"

The back window suddenly exploded and safety glass shattered, completely blinding Bolan's view of their pursuers. Bits of glass rained into the interior, but most of the back window held. In recent years, car manufacturers had been urged by engineers to put safety glass in all vehicle windows, not just the windshield. Some had taken to this practice and others hadn't, so they were fortunate in this case that Bolan had picked a rental with such features. The Executioner hadn't really expected to need them under these circumstances.

"Get the wheel," Bolan ordered Gagliardi. "Head for the highway. We need some running room."

Gagliardi immediately complied, not asking how to do it but simply making the transition gracefully. Bolan slid past him, crawled into the backseat and unsheathed his KA-BAR. Bolan strategically inserted the knife blade in an upper corner, wrapped the sheeted glass around it and then began to twist.

The maneuver pulled the glass away smoothly and soon Bolan had it mostly removed. The rush of wind howled through the interior as Gagliardi climbed the interstate ramp and merged with traffic.

The I-10 wasn't too busy at this time on a Sunday morning, so Bolan figured at least they had that to their advantage. With some running room, he could work more efficiently. The sedan kept pace with them and even started to gain over the distance. At those speeds, the engine in the pursuit car obviously far outmatched that of the rental, and it would take cunning from here on if they expected to shake the followers.

Bolan un-slung his MP-5SD3 and set it to burst mode, then steadied it on the rear dash and leaned his shoulder into the stock. He took a deep breath and as he let it out slowly and steadily, he squeezed off the first trio. A spark on the grill of the sedan rewarded Bolan. Steam immediately belched from the vehicle and a moment later dark smoke started to seep from the edges of the hood. Bolan sighted on the vulnerability and triggered another burst, then a third. The smoke began to roil from the engine, the internal parts obviously trashed as oil and other fluids began to pour from the fatal wounds to the engine block.

The chase car soon dropped back and rolled toward the shoulder, and the gap between them rapidly widened.

Bolan relaxed but the celebration was short-lived. A bright red pickup truck merged onto the highway directly ahead of them, and as they passed the entrance where it had appeared, two more vehicles got on their tail.

"They're trying to box us in," Bolan said.

When Gagliardi didn't reply, Bolan turned and noted he had the cell phone pressed to his ear. At some point during the past few minutes, he had used Bolan's cell and now he was shouting at the top of his lungs that they needed help.

"I don't *give* a good damn if it's Sunday!" Gagliardi said. "You telling me you can't hear what kind of shit is going down at my end? Now get my handler on the phone and do it *now!*"

Bolan's eyes locked with Gagliardi's in the rearview mirror.

"Bureaucrats!" the DEA agent spat.

The Executioner wanted to laugh at that comment but knew it probably wasn't the appropriate time. Gagliardi's heated quip and sarcasm reminded him very much of a certain blond hothead named Carl Lyons. Lyons, head of Stony Man's Able Team—a trio of hard-nosed urban commandos with a penchant for kicking ass wherever the mission took them—had joined Bolan's cause years ago. Back then, the young LAPD sergeant had sported a couple of opportunities to bring Bolan down. But Lyons hadn't been able to move past the idealism of Bolan's war against the Mob; even if he didn't believe it was right, Lyons knew that somebody had to do it. To not give the Executioner at least a fighting chance was the greater crime, to Lyons's way of thinking. Carl "Ironman" Lyons became Bolan's first choice as leader of Able Team. He had a temper, yeah, but he was cool under fire. Methodical.

Bolan saw some of those traits in Gagliardi, and he had to admit it impressed him a bit.

"Stay on it," Bolan said.

Gagliardi waved at the truck ahead of them. "What about these guys?"

"You worry about the wheel, I'll worry about the Zetas," Bolan replied. "Get alongside that truck."

Gagliardi did as instructed, hammering the gas pedal to the floor and whipping into the car-pool express lane until he'd come alongside them. Bolan swept the muzzle of the MP-5SD3 in corkscrew fashion, peppering the truck with rounds. The driver swerved to avoid the sudden assault and the return fire from a couple of Los Zetas guns went high and wide. Bolan switched tactics, turning the submachine gun on the truck's tires. The double blowout caused the driver to lose control and the vehicle careened off the highway and finished with a barrel roll perpetuated by the guard rail.

The two sedans pressed them, attempting to reclaim some of the lost distance. They were nearly on top of Bolan and Gagliardi when out of nowhere a blue-and-white vehicle with flashing lights joined the unsanctioned rally. Bolan immediately recognized the Arizona DPS cruiser. Either the trooper happened to see what was going down or the word was being passed. In any case, it worried Bolan because the cop might not know what he was getting into.

Bolan observed one of the high-end sedans drop back while the other zipped ahead of the DPS cruiser. He watched as a barrel suddenly protruded from the window of the tail vehicle. Bolan could tell the officer was focused on the sedan ahead of him, figuring the other vehicle to be an innocent bystander.

The Executioner triggered the MP-5SD3 but only a single round left the barrel before the bolt locked back on an empty magazine. Bolan tossed the weapon aside and quick drew his Desert Eagle. He leveled the .44 Magnum in a two-fisted grip, sighted on the lead vehicle just to the right of the barrel and squeezed off two successive rounds. The first one sparked off the A-post of the rear sedan but the second landed on target. The barrel disappeared from view and a pink cloud burst from the side of the car, a clear indicator Bolan had bagged the enemy with a head shot.

There was little doubt in Bolan's mind that the DPS officer now had some inkling of who the friendlies were in this situation. Of course, the mere fact Bolan had taken out the shooter didn't mean the cop knew he'd been spared sudden death, but the warrior figured it might go a way toward making the officer rethink the situation and at least pick one side or the other. Bolan's tactic had an impact, somehow, because the officer immediately veered into the open lane and sped past the lead sedan.

He tried to get his cruiser between the enemy car and the

rental, but every time he made the attempt they came dangerously close to hitting one another. An impact at these speeds wouldn't have resulted in a win for either side and everyone involved knew that much. Bolan turned and ordered Gagliardi to take the next exit.

The Executioner figured the time had come to bring this race to a close, and pen the enemy up somewhere he could end this once and for all.

Gagliardi did as instructed and soon they were out of the Phoenix city limits and entering the suburb of Tempe. Gagliardi got off at Elliott Road just off the I-10 at the section known as the Maricopa Freeway, and took a hard right at the bottom of the ramp. As Bolan had hoped, their speeds dropped considerably and this area was mostly commercial. The vast array of businesses along here weren't open yet, so traffic remained light. The four cars continued up the divided four-lane road and eventually the businesses gave way to residences and the road merged to a single lane, divided, that looped toward the east. Off to the south, Bolan noted the rugged terrain.

"Gagliardi, where's this road lead?" Bolan asked.

"It just swings around in a big loop."

"We need to ditch this thing, get some open ground. Any ideas?"

"I was just thinking that myself," Gagliardi said. "There's a massive arroyo up ahead. I figure we could ground there and gain some sort of position."

"Don't forget we have a cop on us now."

"Make that several," Gagliardi said as two Tempe police squads approached on the other side of the divided highway, lights flashing and sirens wailing.

"We don't get this shut down soon, we're going to end up in a shoot-out with the cops," Bolan observed.

Through clenched teeth Gagliardi said, "I'm working on it."

As if on cue, the bridge spanning the arroyo loomed ahead.

Bolan sat facing forward and braced himself, already attuned to what Gagliardi had in mind. The guy seemed comfortable at the wheel, but he had an edge to him and he'd been subjected to enough of a beating that Bolan had to wonder if the guy still had all his marbles intact. A moment later, it didn't seem to matter much as he swerved violently off the road, took out a privacy fence bordering the backyard of a private residence and continued along a stretch of dry, brown grass until they hit the edge of the arroyo.

"Hang on!" he cried to Bolan as he hit the brakes and the vehicle skidded over the edge and jounced its way down the rough terrain.

They hit the bottom of the arroyo and Bolan immediately urged Gagliardi to gain speed for the other side, pulling out a fresh magazine from the butt pack and slamming it home in the MP-5SD3. Gagliardi handled the job like a pro and soon they were climbing up the other side of the arroyo. When they were near the top, the guy slammed on the brakes and skidded to a halt with perfect timing so that the back of the vehicle swung a 180-degree turn and they were facing nose toward the bottom of the arroyo.

Bolan leaped from the vehicle and set up a firing solution as the two sedans followed Gagliardi's wild trail through the poor citizen's backyard and descended the slope. As the enemy vehicles reached the bottom, Bolan triggered a full-auto salvo from the submachine gun. A storm of 9 mm slugs punched through the glass and metal of the Los Zetas vehicles with punishing effect, and the sudden ambush took them by surprise. The drivers did the only thing they could, because neither was carrying enough speed to make the other side—they tried to fan out. Unfortunately, their tires had trouble getting purchase and quickly bogged down in the deep, mushlike sand of the arroyo floor.

Bolan grinned at Gagliardi's ingenuity. Obviously a native of the area, Gagliardi had understood that if they could get the Los Zetas into such a position and execute an assault at their weakest point, they could bring this thing to a stop. The strategy had worked beautifully, and the approaching army of police squads would be enough to dissuade the Zetas from trying to battle their way out of a particularly hopeless situation.

When the bolt locked back on another empty magazine, Bolan said, "I think we've out-stayed our welcome."

"Agreed," Gagliardi said.

The men jumped into the rented sedan, Gagliardi repositioning himself behind the wheel as Bolan took shotgun. As Gagliardi steered out of their position and proceeded along the narrow track that followed the arroyo, Bolan checked behind them to see the squads come to a halt at the top of the arroyo. The two sedans occupied by the Los Zetas gunners were still trying to work their way free but to no avail. Bolan watched as an army of cops arrived and started swarming the area, one group of officers covering with their weapons while another descended the arroyo on foot to take the Los Zetas crew into custody.

"That ought to buy us a little time," Bolan said.

"I don't feel too hot."

Bolan turned and looked at Gagliardi, and immediately noticed a grayish hue to his skin. Beads of sweat stood out on his forehead. Bolan looked him over more carefully and that's when he saw it. The DEA agent was bleeding from his right thigh.

"You've been hit," he said. "Pull over."

Gagliardi looked down and saw the blood now. "I'll be okay, I can hang a little longer."

Bolan clamped a hand on his shoulder. "Pull over, Vince. Do it!"

Something in Bolan's voice obviously had impact, or maybe Gagliardi realized he was talking sense. Either way, Gagliardi did as he was told and Bolan immediately retrieved his butt pack. He pulled the first-aid kit from it, applied a bulky dressing to the man's thigh and then bandaged it tightly.

As he wrapped the wound, he said, "Looks like it went clean through. But we need to get you to a hospital."

"Okay," Gagliardi replied. More quietly he added, "Hey, Cooper?"

"Yeah?"

"Thanks. Thanks for coming after me, man."

"You would have done the same," Bolan replied. "But you're welcome."

"So how did you find me anyway?"

"You wouldn't believe me if I told you."

BOLAN FOUND A MAJOR HOSPITAL ten minutes from their position, and through some bit of good fortune he got Gagliardi there just in time.

"He's lost a lot of blood," the E.R. doc reported. "But he'll be okay."

Bolan made himself scarce once he'd heard Gagliardi would pull through, as he didn't want to get caught up in answering a whole bunch of uncomfortable questions. Besides, he'd reported Gagliardi's credentials to the hospital so the police and an army of DEA agents would arrive here very soon.

And while one phone call to Stony Man Farm could have pulled him out of any legal or political scrape in which he found himself, right at the moment he couldn't afford to be detained. Things had heated to the boiling point and at this critical juncture it was anyone's guess how his latest encounter with Los Zetas would shake out. Both sides were scrambling to respond to a perceived threat by the opposition. The leaders of the two groups were nervous, panicked even, and panicked men could quickly become irrational. The Executioner had been trying to avert a war between the two factions, but it seemed all he'd done was escalate it.

Or at least escalate the timetable.

Bolan had set the pace, pushed his enemies to the brink. He realized it could have dangerous consequences, but he also realized he couldn't have held back from helping Gagliardi. He had to get up and look at himself in the mirror, and Bolan's sense of obligation to friends or comrades sometimes took precedence over his strategy. Leave no man behind. Bolan had held on to the mantra of the U.S. Army Rangers and many other such similar groups. He couldn't stand by and let Gagliardi become another victim.

He had enough ghosts on his conscious.

Bolan found a pay phone and dialed Captain Joseph Hall.

"Yeah?" Hall snapped into the phone midway through the first ring.

"It's me."

"Are you *trying* to give me a heart attack, Cooper? Huh? Is that what you're trying to do? You keep this up and they're gonna have to come roll me up in a straitjacket!"

Bolan kept his voice even. "I told you things were going to heat up."

"Heat up? You know they got a fully equipped SWAT unit *and* a special ops team out looking for you right now? They have your description and the... Hold on a sec." Hall tried to cover the receiver but Bolan could still make out muffled conversation. "What? Okay, okay, I'll look it over in a minute. Thanks. And close the door on your way out. I don't need the whole damned department listening in on my phone calls." Then his voice came back full-on. "You still there, Cooper?"

"Still here," Bolan said.

"Looks like your hunch about that young girl was right."

"How's that?"

"A street unit spotted her about an hour ago, apparently wandering around in a daze. Her name is Claudia Pacorbo, street name of Angel. She's been turning tricks for the high-society types last six years. Been in a lot of trouble, multiple arrests for prostitution. Somebody had worked her over pretty good, but she had a wad of cash and a note telling her to take the money and split town. It was signed only 'Maldo.' Ring any bells?"

"Not off-hand," Bolan said.

"Well, she just split because we couldn't really hold her on anything. I think I'm going to have her tailed, though, see where she goes."

"Understood. Now listen because I only have enough time to run this down once for you. The guys chasing us were all members of Los Zetas. There's a cop at the Chandler Regional Medical Center, a DEA agent who was undercover for sixteen months with that crew. I went in to get him out and things turned hard fast."

"So what do you expect?" Hall said. "You got these guys nervous and they're starting to shoot at anything that moves."

"I'm not surprised, Hall," Bolan answered. "I'm concerned. Concerned that somebody knows about me, maybe even about our little deal."

"What are you suggesting?"

"Nothing. I'm not in the habit of speculating without hard intelligence to back it." Anything less was a waste of time. "I'm telling you to be careful. There could be someone inside your department who isn't so friendly. We both know these cartels have deep pockets, deep enough to tempt even the most stand-up guys. I've seen underpaid cops go wrong before. Somebody burned my DEA friend's cover, and I'm going to find out who. In the meantime, I'm advising you to watch yourself and not trust anybody."

"Well…I got to trust *somebody,* Cooper."

"You can trust me, Hall. That's about all at this point until I know exactly how this agent got burned. Both sides of this equation have to know by now that they're not fighting each other. They know there's a third player, and they know who to look for. If I can get them to focus on me rather than each other, that should be enough for me to draw them away from your operations so you can tighten the noose."

"Well that's good news," Hall said, his voice changing somewhat. "We finally got one of those goons to roll over on his friends, and I got about a half-dozen warrants in the works right now. My only concern is—"

His voice dropped off, and Bolan prompted, "What?"

"Well, I'm worried now that we're going to cross paths. I'd hate for you to get in the line of fire, Cooper."

"Don't worry about that. I told you once I stirred the hornet's nest that you'd be able to take over, and I meant it. My priorities have shifted. I need to find out who's passing intelligence to both sides. They're playing two ends against the middle."

"And *you're* the middle?"

"Exactly."

"All right, fair enough. When can I next expect to hear from you?"

"Hard to tell until I can run down this information leak. I don't know how long that's going to take, and whatever falls out from that will push me toward my next course of action."

"Well, try to get back to me some time tomorrow morning. We're going to execute these warrants at dusk, hit them all at the same time."

"I'll do what I can," Bolan replied. "Good luck."

"You, too…soldier."

The term surprised Bolan coming from a straitlaced, hardnosed cop like Hall, but the guy had disconnected before he could remark on it. Bolan replaced the receiver slowly and returned to his vehicle.

The Executioner had a rat to exterminate.

And he knew *exactly* where to start looking.

7

Hector Casco had a dilemma—one that left him with murder on his heart.

Casco had long ago tried to lift himself out of his primitive roots, to elevate standards and wear a reputation as a businessman. Unfortunately, this latest set of events had left that garment in tatters and he was quickly seeing that he'd have to revert to older methods, tried and true methods, to overcome these latest developments.

Casco could remember back to the time when this enigmatic meddler—the man who dressed up like some kind of soldier but wasn't fooling anybody—had all but destroyed the Carillo cartel. Since that time, many had tried to take Carillo's place, to no avail. The Gulf and Sinaloa cartels were now the two most powerful players, and even that balance of power tipped to and fro like a dinghy on a stormy sea. One day, the Gulf gained the advantage; the next, and the Sinaloa had control again.

Casco muttered curses. This was *not* what he needed at this time. He'd attempted to contact the Gulf leader's second, basically Casco's equal in the ranks, but so far Jorge Cárdonas hadn't responded to the message delivered to his competitors via Casco's most trusted courier. What made matters worse was that Casco wasn't sure upon whom he could rely outside of himself. Maldo had been brooding ever since his return from disposing of the Pacorbo whore. Casco couldn't understand that—it wasn't like he'd ever known his security chief to be squeamish. How many men had the guy readily eliminated without so much as a twitch? Maybe it was some deep-seated psychological thing about doing females. Well that was just too goddamned bad. This was war, and war called for extreme measures.

Casco sat in his office and considered his next move. Whatever it was, it had to be *logical*. He needed to develop a strategy, something Jose Carillo hadn't done when going against this man that the common ranks chose to dub with the title *el Diablo en Negro*: the Devil in Black. Word had just reached Casco less than an hour earlier that Los Zetas had also encountered the bastard, and the guy somehow had led them into a trap sprung by the cops. It made Casco wonder—was the Devil in Black working with the police?

Everything Casco knew about the guy suggested he operated alone, although he'd been known to work in concert with the DEA. He'd certainly had support when fighting the Carillo cartel, and there were rumors he'd gone up against more than fifty Colombian FARC soldiers and reduced them to shambles single-handedly. Okay, so Casco could buy that this man was very dangerous, but he was still flesh and blood and that meant he was susceptible to all the same weaknesses as any man.

What Casco deemed most interesting was the man's apparent concern for the bystanders. In every instance it had been touted how very selective this individual was. Those not the target of his operations, particularly innocent types or just people going about their daily routine, were usually nowhere near the action. Maybe it was coincidence but Casco found that difficult to believe. If nothing else, the Devil in Black had shown a weakness for bystanders, and Casco figured the best strategy at this point would be to exploit that weakness.

Casco whipped the house phone off its receiver. "Maldo, get in here and bring two heads with you."

A smiled played at his lips as Casco replaced the phone. Yes, he knew exactly what kind of strategy to employ, one that would bring this meddling prick right to his doorstep. And it would be perfect.

THE EXECUTIONER STOOD in the shadows of the alley and watched the pharmacy entrance.

It was nearing 1200 hours, and the place would be opening shortly, according to the sign on the window. Nothing appeared to be happening, though, and hadn't since Bolan's arrival more than an hour earlier. Nobody had even arrived to open the place, and for a moment he began to wonder if Hall's team closed the place down after their raid went awry.

Somehow, Bolan couldn't buy it.

The information Gagliardi had given the Executioner, prompting him to check it out in the first place, seemed like solid intelligence. Had it not been for Hall nearly walking into an ambush here, Bolan might have been able to obtain the information he sought. This was his only remaining lead, and Bolan didn't see anything wrong with tapping the edge of the hole one more time to see what creature popped its head up for a look. Activity on the street was still pretty dead. Bolan marked a couple of places on the street where the bodies of several Los Negros gang members had breathed their last breaths. The city had cleaned up most of the mess but a few bloodstains were still mildly visible if he looked hard enough.

For a moment, Bolan could only experience deep empathy. He took no pleasure in doing what he had to do. He never had. While he'd worn his "Executioner" moniker without complaint during his military service, and he'd carried the title with

him into the Mafia war and beyond, Bolan had also borne
another name: Sergeant Mercy. It wasn't for any compassion
shown toward the enemy—such feelings would have put him
six feet under long ago—but that which he showed toward
the civilians on both sides.

Bolan had also never dropped the hammer on a cop, view-
ing them as soldiers of the same side. He had, on occasion,
terminated cops who had allied themselves with the enemy.
But police officers operating in the course of their duties, like
a patrolman, detectives or members of special units? No…
never. He'd never stoop to such predatory tendencies, because
that difference was all that stood between him and those he
fought. It was a thin wire to walk, sure, but Bolan would
gladly do it because he saw it as his duty. Beside, his hands
weren't tied as guys like Joe Hall's were—Bolan could and
would fight back with everything at his disposal.

The flicker of sunlight on metal caught his eye, and the
door to the pharmacy opened. The massive wrought-iron gate
rolled up a moment later, and a hulking form emerged from
the shadows. The guy wore jeans and a blue-and-purple vest—
the colors of the pharmacy—over a black t-shirt. A plethora
of tattoos snaked along his beefy arms, and his shaved head
shone in the sunlight. The stock clerk look to which he aspired
might have fooled some, but Bolan's practiced eye dissolved
the facade in a moment.

This guy was a Sinaloa hardcase, period.

Bolan left the alley and crossed the fifty odd feet in
seconds.

The big dude almost didn't see him coming, but at the last
second he turned and locked eyes with Bolan. The Executioner was on him before the guy could react—Bolan grabbed
the front of his shirt and dragged him toward the still open
doorway of the pharmacy. The very large man wasn't used
to being accosted and tried to pull Bolan's grip free. He had
no idea he was going up against a warrior of both superior

skill and strength. When Bolan grabbed hold of an opponent, brute strength alone wouldn't pry him off.

When they were inside, Bolan closed the door behind him with a backward kick and then hauled the bruiser across the room. The guy hit his rib cage on the edge of the counter and produced a grunt. He recovered quickly and turned on Bolan, swinging a ham-sized fist in a looping punch that Bolan saw coming long before it became a threat. The soldier stepped inside close and threw up both hands, one connecting with a major nerve in the man's bicep, the other contacting the side of his neck. He immediately followed with a knee to the groin, and as the man bent over, Bolan clamped his palms across the enemy's ears.

The massive hardcase dropped like a stone to the polished linoleum floor.

The guy started to get to his feet but the cold metal of the Beretta 93-R muzzle against his ear changed his mind.

"Whad'ya want?" the man said thickly, still dazed by Bolan's assault.

"Information."

"I ain't telling you shit."

"That's a very poor attitude," Bolan said, stepping off the guy, but watching him carefully. He didn't plan to get caught off guard. "And here I thought we were off to a good start."

"Why should I tell you anything, *pinche*." The man raised his head to look at Bolan. "You're just going to kill me."

Bolan produced a cool smile. "If I wanted you dead, you would be. I wouldn't have come in here playing nice."

"I ain't no rat. And I don't talk to no cops."

"I'm not a cop," Bolan said. "Although I'm sure I could arrange a meeting."

"Fuck off and die, pig. I can smell cops a mile away."

"Let's move on to something else," Bolan said with a sigh.

The hood let out a scoffing laugh. "You deaf or something,

man? I told you already I wasn't saying nothin'. Besides, you don't know who you're fuckin' with, homes. You just crossed a line you can't uncross."

"Yeah, I figure I've already sort of done that a few times. The experience was overrated."

Something on the order of recognition suddenly crossed the man's dark features, and his eyes glittered a moment. "Oh, man, I know who you are. Dude, you are totally wiped. There's a price on your head so large you ain't going to be able to take a shit in this town without someone lookin' to cap your ass."

"Well, that's funny," Bolan said in an impassive tone. "That just so happens to be what I want to talk about. Is it Hector Casco?"

"Who?"

"Don't play me for stupid. I'm not in the mood. I know this place is a front operation for Hector Casco, and I know you and every other punk in here works for him. Somebody set up an ambush for the cops here yesterday. What do you know about that?"

"I ain't saying *shit*, hombre. Don't you get it?"

"I get it," Bolan said. He clipped the guy behind the ear with the butt of the pistol and knocked him cold. He cinched the man's hands behind him with a pair of plastic riot cuffs.

Bolan looked around the lower level of the pharmacy but didn't see anything to draw his attention. Well, it was a three-story building, so there had to be more than just this first floor. It took a bit of doing but eventually he found a door in the back. There were steps beyond this point, and Bolan ascended them with the Beretta held ahead of him. Only a single, dim bulb at the top landing illuminated the narrow stairwell. Bolan reached the second floor unmolested.

The Executioner began a sweep of each room along the second floor hallway, but found all of them empty save one. This room had been converted into a studio apartment, which included a bed, kitchenette and portable desk with a computer notebook on it. Bolan moved over to the desk and tapped a key on the laptop; the screen shimmered to life as the hard drive whirled up with a muted hum. Bolan noted the computer was unlocked.

A quick dig through a number of electronic files provided more information than he could have hoped for. There wasn't time for him to sift through all of it, but he knew somebody who could. Bolan noted the laptop had a wireless connection device attached, so he unplugged it from the wall and retraced his steps to the first floor with the laptop in hand.

The big man was still unconscious as Bolan stepped past him and made for the exit.

"LOOKS LIKE YOU HIT a gold mine, Striker," Aaron Kurtzman said.

"Some good news is welcome," Bolan replied. "How's it break down, Bear?"

"Well, according to what you sent me, these are sales and distribution reports for a number of offshore investment firms backing a manufacturing company. The company is conveniently located just across the border on the Mexican side of Nogales. I'm sure that comes as a huge surprise to you."

Bolan chuckled. "Loss for words."

"Thought so," Bear replied with an infectious laugh of his own. "Anyway, it would appear on the surface that this manufacturing plant has nothing to do with Hector Casco."

"What do you mean?"

"His name's not on it anywhere. I'm guessing this little business he's running is a paper company and he's using the factory to smuggle drugs into the country. It's no secret Casco's as dirty as they come. He's been arrested a few times, mostly petty offenses, and one grand jury indictment seven years ago that went nowhere because the prosecution's one and only witness disappeared. A judge threw it out of court after Casco's lawyers filed an MTD."

"If his legal representation didn't get him off, a nice healthy bribe would have."

"I can't argue with that."

"What else can you tell me?"

Kurtzman gave him the address of the factory. "I've pulled up the layout of the physical plant. You want me to send it along?"

"Yeah, you can transmit to my phone."

"Hey, Striker, how are things going down there?"

"What do you mean?"

"Well, it sounds like you got your hands full. I know it's not an *official* mission but Hal and Barb wanted me to let you know that we're standing by to send some support if you need it."

Bolan considered the offer a moment. He might have been able to use Jack Grimaldi, Stony Man's ace flier and one of Bolan's oldest allies, but he couldn't be sure Grimaldi wasn't already off on some other mission with Able Team or Phoenix Force. He could sense they only wanted to help, but he also felt this was one mission he had to complete on his own.

"Tell them I appreciate the offer, Bear," Bolan said. "But I started this solo and I intend to finish it that way."

"Well…just so you know the offer stands."

"Got it."

"What else can I tell you about Casco that might help?"

"Known associates?"

"It's pretty thin there. I'm afraid these files don't contain much in the way of personnel information. I would imagine most of that is kept under lock and key. I can tell you what we have from DEA."

"I've already got that. Speaking of which, can you do me a favor? Can you crack into the DEA's computer files for me?

Get me anything you can on the handler for Vincent Gagliardi, a field agent operating out of the Phoenix office."

"Anything specifically you're looking for?"

"Nothing maybe. Just running down a hunch."

"I put more faith in your hunches than I do some scientific facts, Striker."

"Don't break out the champagne yet," Bolan quipped. "Any chance Casco might be doing more at that factory than just shuttling drugs?"

"Such as?"

"There's a big business in cooking these days, particularly given the demands on crack cocaine and other similar substances. It's also become popular for the creation of designer drugs. It brings twice the price for half the usual product, and it takes a lot of the risk out of running local labs."

"You're suggesting maybe Casco's able to do a bigger business in Phoenix and surrounding areas while crunching out the competition?"

"Right."

"Sounds like a pretty plausible theory."

"And it happens to explain why Casco hasn't been caught so far. Casco's a businessman when you come right down to it. He's not going to dirty his hands and he certainly isn't going to risk his entire operation trusting locals. Suppose he's using the factory to cook meth. It's a decent front operation, and he doesn't have to worry about trouble from competitors. He'll also get the full cooperation of the government because the manufacturing plant is providing jobs."

"If you're right, Striker, that kind of business would mean millions to Casco."

"It would also secure his position in the Southwest. He'd be able to outdistribute his competitors, particularly the Gulf cartel."

"That'll get them hot under the collar. They'll put a price on his head for sure."

"I can tell you they did that long ago. But something still bugs me about all of this."

"And that is?"

"Casco's name doesn't seem to go on anything, Bear. In fact, he's never been seen in public, that I know of. The only photograph I've seen of him came out of a DEA file, and that one was taken by Mexican police during a juvenile arrest. It's at least fifteen years old. Casco could look much different these days. Do me a favor and keep digging. I need to get something solid on this guy before it's too late."

"Roger that."

"And Bear?"

"Yeah?"

"Tell Hal and Barb thanks again. This is just something I need to do alone."

"You bet, Striker. Good hunting."

8

In spite of the fact it was Sunday morning, the office of Arizona Governor Elizabeth Kampp buzzed with harried staff while a growing press corps waited on the fringes of the state capitol building. The governor sat in her office and stared out the window, wistful for the simpler times when she served in the state senate—meet a couple of months out of the year, approve the budget and that was it. The rest of the time she spent with her family, or traveling and campaigning.

Kampp wouldn't have admitted it to anyone, but she resented her political ambitions as of late and her decision to run for the governorship. Had she to do it over, Kampp would have stayed put. She'd had a good career in the legislature—passed a lot of good bills, and earned the respect and loyalty of her constituents. Not only was she a woman, but she was also the fifth woman to be governor of Arizona—more than any other state in the country—with a better reputation for positive change than her predecessors. Not that they hadn't all done well while in office, but she'd been declared a model for smart and ambitious women everywhere, and some of her closest aides and supporters had suggested she consider running for the U.S. presidency. That idea scared her to death and she dismissed it as quickly as it had been suggested, although she'd done so with dignity and in a joking fashion. Some staunch supporters were not easily dissuaded, however, and a couple came back with a vow of support for a shot as vice president. Again, she turned down their generous offers and now that she was experiencing her taste at the top, if the governorship of this state could be considered such, she didn't regret the decision.

Since taking office the previous year it had been one nightmare followed by another. The budget was completely off the charts, the legislature did more squabbling than voting and the bureaucrats and contributors had recently started calling in some of the favors that put her in the chair. Never mind crime and poverty were on the rise with the economic downturn, and it looked as if Arizona would maintain its status quo as kidnap capital of the world.

A soft rap on the doorjamb broke her daydreaming. "Governor?"

Kampp turned, a little startled, but her shoulders relaxed when she saw her chief aide standing at the door. Beau Hastings was as gay as they came, his lithe form attired in slacks and a short sleeve pink shirt with a light gray tie and sleeveless vest to complete the ensemble. He'd been a fantastic personal aide when Kampp served in the legislature and she'd brought him along when elected to this position.

"Sorry, Beau, I was sort of zoning out. What is it?"

Hastings stepped into the room and closed the door enough to give them a little privacy. He padded across the office carpet, holding out the papers like a football receiver running stiff-armed toward the goal line.

"Just set them on my desk. What are they?"

"They're mostly reports from the HIKE squad."

"The who?"

"The anti-kidnapping team of the Phoenix police?"

"Oh, yes…*them*."

The Home Invasion and Kidnapping Enforcement squad

was led by a hard-nosed and often belligerent captain named Joseph Hall. Kampp had met him on only one occasion, and immediately pegged him as a first-class jerk. She'd actually considered asking the police chief to replace him but ultimately opted to stay out of it. That was just more politics and she didn't feel it was right to use her influence to turn a guy out simply because he wasn't Mr. Saturday Night. Besides, Hall had an excellent record of service, more than fifteen years with a number of meritorious citations and commendations. Not to mention he held a medal of valor—the highest decoration a police officer could earn—that was usually awarded posthumously.

And it wasn't like Hall didn't get *any* results. The rise in kidnappings was only a sign of increased resources and activity on the part of the criminal enterprises that committed them, and really not an indicator of ineffective policing. The Phoenix Police Department was doing the very *best* that it could to reign in the horrific goings-on, and they were doing it on a very tight budget with shortages in every area of their operations. Kampp had sent word to the White House, requesting additional financial aid. She'd even invited the president to come out and see what was happening, but he'd been called to more pressing matters and sent the assistant director of the Justice Department to assist.

Hah! What a joke that turned out to be. The ADJD sat on his fat rump, sucking down the free hors d'oeuvres and booze and commenting with grunts like some sort of gorilla in between licking his thumbs and fingers. By the time their meeting had ended, Kampp felt like a complete idiot. Sure, the guy had nodded and agreed that something had to be done, and how he was going to go back to his people and start kicking butts to get some action. Nothing happened. Three months went by and Kampp had Beau send an email on her behalf. Six months came and went, so Kampp finally picked up the phone and called him. She left messages but he never returned her calls. It was only when she went over his head that her office finally received a formal letter of apology and a guarantee they were looking into the situation. She heard nothing else and finally gave up.

"Meanwhile, our citizens continue to get seized off our streets or right out of their homes, and we seem powerless to do anything about it," Kampp told her husband in bed one night.

"You'll get it fixed, honey," he assured her. "Your children and I believe in you."

She knew he was only trying to be supportive, which was pretty sweet considering he'd been somewhat against her running for governor. Oh, he'd never come right out and said it but she knew just by the look in his eyes when she'd told him of her plans to submit her candidacy. For a brief moment something had changed in his expression, but then he just nodded and smiled. That was the most infuriating thing about Henry and yet it's what she loved most about him. He was quiet but never brooding, often sad that he didn't get more of her attention but never complained.

Her parents had tried to dissuade her from marrying the young ASU chemistry professor. After all, she came from practically royal blood with a father and grandfather who had served in the high politics of Arizona all their lives. Kampp had never thought about doing anything else from the time she was a little girl—politics was in her family heritage, in her blood. She'd found the huge assembly rooms grand and sweeping, and had taken great pleasure in accompanying her father to the legislative sessions every now and then. She'd listen with rapt attention while men—and women—stood up and delivered wonderful speeches to defend their positions.

Even then Kampp *knew* what she wanted to do.

"Elizabeth, I…" Hastings's voice faded.

"What is it, Beau?" She smiled at him. "You know you can speak freely when we're alone."

"I just didn't want to overstep my bounds."

"Don't worry, if you overstep I'll let you know."

"Yes, ma'am." Hastings continued to hesitate and then it came gushing out of him. "It's just that, I'm very concerned for the safety of the people. Everybody, in fact, and I do include myself in that group. Governor, the citizens of this great state have put their trust and faith in you, believing that you will execute whatever is in their best interests. But lately I've noticed you seem almost resigned, as if you don't care…which I know isn't true, because you've always been a caring person, so I'm not saying that you don't care, please understand. But it really bothers me that *other* people think that you don't care, and you know I try not to listen to the rumors that float around, but it's so difficult when people say things in earshot even though they think you *can't* hear them. And well, it's just very disconcerting for me…that's all…I wanted to say, really." He put his fist on his hip.

"Is that it?" she asked, finding herself utterly unable to contain a bit of amusement at his verve.

"Well, I suppose so. Other than maybe I just wanted you to know that I'm still pulling for you, and you know that I will be…no matter what, but I'm…I'm…"

"What is it, Beau?"

"I'm *scared*, Elizabeth." His eyes glistened. "I'm afraid to walk to my car at the end of the day. I'm afraid to go to the bathroom in a public place. I've taken to walking around my house at least twice to make sure nobody's waiting in the shadows to jump on me when I put my key in the lock. I sit in front of the television with my supper every night, watching sappy movies because I don't want to risk watching the news and seeing something about another kidnapping or murder. Do you know how many times I've watched *Must Love Dogs* and *Titanic*? I could practically quote that last one for you by heart."

"Beau," Kampp said, rising from her chair, walking around

her desk and putting her hands on his shoulders. "I'm not going to let anything happen to you. Okay? We're doing everything we can to put an end to this. The police are working 'round the clock and I'm doing what I can to get FBI involvement, as well. I've moved this back to the White House and at any minute I'm sure that—"

The phone rang, startling them a bit and intruding on what Hastings had considered a very intimate moment shared between them. Kampp knew that he relied on her, more than an aide should, but she'd never done anything to discourage him. She had taken much of a motherly role where it concerned him, although he was his own man and she'd never intruded in his life. He respected her views and resolve, and she respected his.

Kampp picked up the phone midway through the second ring. "Governor Kampp."

"Governor? My name is Harold Brognola, I'm a special envoy with the Justice Department."

"Ah, Mr. Brognola. Thank you for contacting me, although I am expecting a call from the Oval Office. Would there perhaps be an opportune time to call you back?"

"Madam Governor, let me say up front that this *is* your call from the Oval Office."

A long silence followed as Kampp wasn't certain how to react. She had taken some very harsh criticisms for her public show of support of the Washington administration. Kampp had been ensconced with extremely conservative bedfellows since her earliest days in public office, and the fact she'd been verbal about her belief in the president and some of his policies had ruffled the feathers of more than a few supporters in her camp.

Well to hell with them. There were lives at stake here and she didn't have time for pettiness. "I see, sir. Well…will the president not be speaking to me?"

"No, ma'am, as a matter of fact he's sitting right here. And he does want to talk to you but he asked me to open this dialog. Do you have a moment?"

"Of course."

"Governor, I won't mince words. I'm ashamed, personally ashamed, of how you were treated by the Justice Department, and I can give you my assurances that we're dealing with this situation. In fact, you're probably staring at some reports right about now relative to recent actions that have taken place in Phoenix."

"I just got them by courier. I haven't had the chance to look them over."

"I ordered those sent to you directly from the NCIC computers an hour ago."

"Really? I thought they were from the HIKE squad at the Phoenix P.D."

"There are reports on their activities in there, yes. A full disclosure, in fact, and sort of our way of apologizing for the hand-job you've gotten. I beg you to forgive the expression."

"I came up in state politics, Mr. Brognola. I've heard worse. Forget it."

"Very well." Brognola cleared his throat. "So we have a proposal for you. In those reports you will find that there have been some very recent arrests, and the HIKE squad is about to make some more. There have also been a number of...oh, shall we say 'incidents' of violence. I'm happy to report the casualties have been isolated to the bad guys."

"I'm not concerned about dead criminals, sir. I'm concerned about innocent citizens getting caught in the crossfire and missing or dead children. I'm concerned about a public that's panicked by an escalating situation on the short path to being totally out of control. And you know what else, Mr. Brognola? There's an army of press people on my doorstep wanting answers, and all I can tell them is that somebody here is now turning my city into a war zone."

"Oh, I can guarantee you that the man to whom you're referring is doing anything but that."

"You sent this person?"

"Not exactly," Brognola said. "But we're working on sending some additional support his way."

"Mr. Brognola, I don't mean to be a bitch here but I have to tell you that I'm prepared to protect my constituents at any costs. You know that I have the authority to do whatever it takes to quell what I'm deeming to be a statewide emergency at this point. If necessary, I will call up the National Guard and Department of Public Safety Special Response Teams to deal with this if I must. And I will close off the borders of the state to prevent risk to folks traveling through here. I can do it and I *will* do it if my hand is forced."

"I know your authority, Madam Governor. There's no need to threaten me. I'm on *your* side, please remember that. Tell me what I can do to help?"

"Can you send additional law enforcement? Perhaps some officials at the federal level who can keep them on a short leash?"

"I can and will. What else?"

"What about calling off this nut running around shooting gangbangers and driving on our streets like a bat out of hell?"

"I can't speak for that individual directly," Brognola replied. He cleared his throat. "You would, um…have to talk to him personally if you wanted an answer to your question. What I can tell you is that he is your absolute best weapon against the kidnappers and drug pushers. They're the *real* enemies, not this man. He's doing what nobody else can do, and from where I'm sitting he's doing one hell of a job. My most recent information tells me that there are a number of high-ranking members of enforcement groups from both the Sinaloa and Gulf cartels either dead or in custody. Raids are happening all over the city, as we speak. Drug houses and meth labs are being shut down everywhere, and I was recently informed this individual you're concerned about is on the verge of taking out a major pipeline running up to your city from the Mexico side of Nogales."

Kampp took a few seconds to process that bit of news, and then said, "Well, obviously we're making tremendous headway in just a short time. I only wish that someone had bothered to call and tell me it was going to happen."

"I'm calling you now. This is the first and best opportunity I've had to advise you, and probably the reason that the president ordered me to do so."

"You work for the Justice Department, Mr. Brognola? Because it sounds an awful lot like you have a very intimate relationship with the White House."

"I cannot confirm or deny anything about that relationship. But believe that when I say jump, there are few who don't have to ask how high."

"Okay, then I'll take you at your word."

"Thank you," Brognola said. "Please hold for the President of the United States."

"Mr. Brognola," Kampp said with urgency.

"Yes?"

"One other thing. This individual you told me about. Is he really as good as you say he is? Can this man single-handedly take down an entire criminal underworld as large as the Gulf and Sinaloa cartels? I mean, the entire power of the U.S. government hasn't been able to do that, even with all of the money and resources at its disposal."

"Governor Kampp, if just such a man were to exist in the world, it would be this man. I can say with great confidence that he won't let us down. And he won't let *you* down."

"I have some very frightened people on my hands, and I cannot simply say that we're to pin all our hopes on one man. They'll laugh me out of the capitol building."

"It is important that you keep that little bit of information to yourself. Don't tell *anyone*. This is a matter of the highest security."

"You say he won't let us down, fine. But…how do you *know?*"

"Because he's never let us down before," Brognola replied.

9

Bolan's phone demanded his attention. The warrior lowered his binoculars and answered. "Yeah?"

"Striker, it's Barb."

Barbara Price. Yeah. The one woman in the world who had shared both a personal and professional relationship with Bolan and lived to tell about it. Their personal relationship, of late, remained one of pure intimacy and little else. They fulfilled a need for one another, not purely a carnal need, although to the outside observer it might have seemed so, but one born deeper from a need for personal human contact.

The Executioner had maintained a distant if strenuous relationship with his government. When he first created the Stony Man Farm complex with Brognola, and personally hand-selected the core-sensitive operations group—most of whom served to this day—Bolan had wondered how long it would last. If the day ever came when bureaucratic apathy and political corruption facilitated an attack on the Farm, taking Bolan's only true love and resulting in the death of several good men, Bolan would sever all official ties and strike out on his own once more.

For the moment, the fat cats in Washington saw him as little more than a necessary evil. Except for Price and Brognola, and the other people of Stony Man. They still believed in him, believed in his purpose and mission, and were always ready to lend a hand whenever he called on them. In return, Bolan would occasionally act on the behalf of his government when the mission objectives aligned with his own and the Man didn't trust anyone else to get the job done. Over the years since Bolan's estranged relationship with his government, Brognola had offered a truce and tried to return him to the fold.

But the Executioner had never been one to wholly trust the government cog. Sure, he believed in Brognola one hundred percent—as well as those who had dedicated their lives to the War Everlasting along with him—because the guy had never betrayed him. Brognola had never given Bolan a reason to mistrust or doubt him—never lied to him, that he knew of. In fact, Bolan would have believed the Stony Man chief's word over that of just about anybody else he knew.

"What's up?" Bolan asked Price.

"I called to let you know that Bear got the information you requested on that DEA handler. He'll be sending it over to you in a minute."

"You obviously didn't call just to tell me that, Barb," Bolan said lightly.

"No. I also wanted to let you know that Hal talked to the Man and got permission to become officially involved in this matter. We're clear to lend whatever support you need."

Bolan considered that a moment. "I told Bear to ask you guys to stay neutral."

"I know," she said. Price paused a moment and then said, "Listen, Striker, we're…well, it's just that we're concerned about you. You're up against a considerable force down there and without any kind of backup. Hal hates to think you could disappear and we wouldn't have any idea what happened to you. Besides, we wouldn't want you to run short on supplies or equipment. We're sending Jack down if that's okay."

"Has he left yet?"

"He has, as a matter of fact."

"Then I guess it'll have to be okay." He paused and then added, "Thanks. To all of you."

"Don't mention it."

"So what else can you tell me?"

"Well, you might be interested to know we've been running this down ever since you first contacted us. Apparently the noise you made in Phoenix has ruffled some political feathers, not the least of which includes the governor's office."

"I'm sorry to hear that," Bolan said. "But I can't very well be concerned with how this affects someone's campaign contributions."

"Actually, Governor Elizabeth Kampp is a decent lady. Honest and about as tough as they come. You'd probably like her if you met her."

"Maybe."

"Anyway, after the fallout yesterday I guess Captain Joseph Hall took you up on your offer and called Hal. He talked to him for about five minutes and then as soon as they hung up with each other, Hal was on the phone with the Man."

"Funny," Bolan said. "I figured the president would want to shut me down."

"He did…at first. Then Hal ran it down for him, explained the positive results you were getting. When the Man heard you'd started this one on your own, and that a number of major cartel leaders on both sides were going down hard, he changed his tune and offered his full support. Hal's already been on the phone with Governor Kampp and made certain assurances that you'll act with discretion, but also asked that she cut you some slack."

"She going to back off?"

"Hal seems to think so. Wait a minute…he's back now, so I'll let him tell you himself. I'm going to put you on speaker."

There was a click followed by silence, and then Brognola's voice came on strong with just the hint of an echo. "You with us, Striker?"

"I'm here."

"Okay, I know you might be a little aggravated with me for going around your request, but this was one of those times I had no choice. The president got wind of what was happening and I guess he knew immediately you were involved."

"Maybe you found my leak."

"Come again?"

"Never mind. Go on, Hal."

"Okay, well here's an update on the situation. Your little thunderstorm down there the past two days has brought an army of press to Phoenix and put the governor's staff on full alert. We've promised to commit additional law enforcement to the city and surrounding metro areas to help the efforts of this…what do they call it…HIKE squad?"

"Yeah, Hall's a good cop."

"I got that impression from talking with him yesterday," Brognola said. "Believe it or not, though, he's echoed many of the same sentiments as the governor. Not enough money or resources to combat this problem. I told her, as did the Man, that we would do everything in our power to supply her with enough to fill the gap, but that she could maintain autonomy in how to best utilize those resources."

"Let me guess. I was the concession."

"Exactly. She's agreed to look the other way while you pursue whatever angles you need to while you're there. But try not to step on any more toes. And if you have to go back to Phoenix, at least tell Hall so he can keep Governor Kampp appeased. She just wants to make sure they have time to get bystanders free and clear of any potential hot spots."

"I can do that, no sweat," Bolan replied. "But I don't think they're going to have to worry. It seems to me that when I get done hitting this place in Nogales, I won't have to return to Phoenix."

"You think they'll come to you," Brognola concluded.

"You know it. There's no doubt both Casco and his competitors have heard they're not fighting each other. At first that worried me, but I've figured out how to use it to my advantage."

Price said, "You think if they're focused on you, and not each other, that'll draw them away from their activities in Phoenix. And that distraction might buy Hall and his people enough time to excise them little by little."

"You got it," Bolan said.

"Well merry Christmas, then, because your plan seems to be working," Brognola said. "According to the intelligence we just pulled, the HIKE squad has neutralized about a half-dozen locations just off the information you funneled to them."

"Not to mention they've made three dozen or so arrests of known operators associated with both cartels," Price added.

"That's good work on their part," Bolan agreed.

"They couldn't have done it without you, Striker," Brognola countered in a matter-of-fact tone.

"Thanks, Hal, but let's not hand out any awards yet. We still have a long way to go on this."

The rumble of a giant diesel engine drew Bolan's attention. He looked up and saw a semitrailer approaching the complex slowly. This was the moment he'd been waiting for.

"It would seem opportunity knocks," Bolan told Brognola. "I need to run. Where's Eagle going to meet me?"

"Well, there's Nogales International Airport about seven miles north of the business district in Santa Cruz County," Price said. "It was closed to commercial aviation effective May 2009 for security reasons given its proximity to the port of entry."

"Fine, let him know I'll meet him there when I'm through with this."

"Take care, Striker," Brognola said.

"Out, here."

The Executioner clicked off and then raised the binoculars to his eyes and followed the course of the slow-moving semitrailer. Bolan was maybe a hundred yards from the dusty, one-lane road that led to the factory entrance. The area had quite a bit of security, including a twelve-foot-high chain-link fence topped with barbed wire, motorized cameras at every corner and a guard station at both gated entrances. Through the binoculars, Bolan had been able to see that the guards carried automatic weapons, not to mention that all of the entrance doors to the facility appeared to require access by coded keycards.

That truck would be his only way in.

Bolan stowed the binoculars and burst from the cover he'd taken behind some rocks and sagebrush. The soldier sprinted across the jagged desert terrain, ignoring the foliage and other geographical hazards tugging at the pants bloused into his boots. Bolan had traded out his blacksuit for more appropriate apparel, a BDU set in a six-color desert-camouflage pattern favored by the American armed forces fighting in desert countries.

The Beretta and Desert Eagle rode in the usual spots, and Bolan had also traded out the MP-5 in favor of his other standard arsenal, the FN-FNC. Manufactured by Fabrique Nationale, Bolan had come to appreciate the FNC for its versatility. It chambered 5.56×45 mm NATO rounds and boasted a rotating bolt design like its predecessor, the CAL, but with a much more stable design. When the stock was folded, as it presently was, the weapon took on a carbine profile at a length of about thirty inches. It had proven its dependability time and again as rugged and reliable under the most varied and adverse conditions.

From his load-bearing equipment harness he'd attached his KA-BAR combat knife taped to one side, the weapon suspended upside down for easy access, and from the other side dangled a couple of M-62 fragmentation grenades. Bolan would have preferred some of the Diehl DM-51 hand bombs, an Austrian-made ordnance that facilitated "modes" of offensive or defensive depending on the situation, but his reserves were dangerously low. It would be good to have Grimaldi arriving in a few short hours in a plane that sported a full-equipped armory.

Bolan reached the road within a few minutes and immediately jumped onto the trailer of the semitrailer. Mounted to the tailgate, Bolan reached to his belt and removed a small grappling line and utility hook. He swung the hook up and onto the roof and pulled hard until the superstrong tines of the hook bit into the metal-and-fiberglass roof of the trailer and caught on its lip. Bolan scaled the line hand over hand, his taut muscles pulling his dominating frame up the rope with ease.

The Executioner reached the top, threw over a leg and pulled his body the rest of the way until he lay prone on the roof. He quickly retrieved the grappler and rope, and returned them to his belt. Bolan hadn't observed any observation towers or guards roaming the roof of the factory and the top of the semitrailer would extend beyond the cameras. They were pointed toward the ground, obviously designed to scan the perimeter and immediate areas just outside. Nobody would expect him entering in this fashion, not to mention he had the element of surprise.

As the truck rounded a turn and the guard shack came into view, Bolan scrambled to the center of the trailer and pressed his cheek to its sun-baked roof. It burned him some but Bolan ignored the pain. As long as he remained flat and utterly still, the aerodynamics shield that arced over the cab of the tractor-trailer would obscure him from the eyes of four armed guards at the front gate.

Bolan froze as the vehicle came to a halt. He couldn't make

out the conversation for the idle of the massive diesel engine, but it sounded brief. The truck remained there for some time and at one point Bolan heard the tailgate rise and felt the vibrations as an unknown number of men inspected the truck's interior and cargo.

Finally, they finished their inspection and Bolan breathed a sigh of relief as he heard the door shut with a clang. He remained motionless for what seemed like hours but was only about ten minutes, give or take. Soon he heard a shout and the next thing he knew the truck was on the move once more and they were passing through the gates. The truck moved along the periphery of the building and eventually rolled to a crawl when it reached the loading docks.

The driver steered the truck into a hard turn, straightened his rear end and then began to back the rig toward the docks. Once parked, Bolan heard him kill the engine; the cab door opened and he detected a pair of feet hitting the ground. There were new voices now, and these he could hear very clearly. They were talking in Spanish and the conversation seemed animated. The voices got louder and then eventually Bolan heard what sounded like a hard object on a soft one.

The grunt of a male was followed by the thud of a body hitting the ground. There was no mistaking it—Bolan knew *that* sound well.

The Executioner couldn't understand why they would have sacked the driver, but he couldn't show his cards yet. He had to know for certain that he was hitting one of Casco's operations. It wouldn't do for him to blow the place to bits only to find out later the business was completely legitimate. He also had to figure out how to get its employees out of the factory without alerting the security to his presence. In other circumstances he might have considered simply finding the meth-processing operation and then blowing the place sky-high, but it was all too possible that there were Mexican citizens working in the plant who knew nothing of Casco's murderous operations.

Bolan could not salve his conscience if he killed innocent civilians along the way. No casualties of war—not in his war anyway. There may have been plenty of blood on Casco's hands but Bolan wouldn't allow it to be on his own, too. He wouldn't stoop to the activities of the vermin he'd come here to eradicate.

Bolan waited until the voices started to fade and risked edging to one side of the trailer. He looked over the side and then toward the rear in time to see two men dragging a third, maybe the driver and maybe not, through a metal door at one end of the dock. They were busy enough with their awkward package not to notice him, and Bolan kept quiet until they disappeared behind the door, which closed with a clang.

As soon as they were gone, Bolan crawled to the other side of the trailer, swung his legs over and slowly eased his body until he hung from the roof by his fingertips. He took a deep breath and then let himself fall to the pavement, exhaling sharply as he landed, then crouched at the end so the shock would dissipate instead of his knees having to absorb it all.

Bolan stood, wiped the dust from his hands and eased to the cab. He snaked his Beretta 93-R from shoulder leather and mounted the lifter step until he could peer into the cab. Empty. Bolan started to dismount the cab and then got an idea. He eased the cab open, reached inside and grabbed the ignition key. If he had to leave in a hurry, it would be good to have some sort of motorized transportation. Maybe it wasn't the fastest ride in the world, but it could do some distance and there was little to get in his way where obstacles were concerned.

Bolan slid the keys in his pocket, closed and secured the cab door, then returned to the pavement. He reached the back of the semitrailer and used the assist rail to ascend to the loading dock platform. Bolan traversed the platform, staying close to the bay doors until he reached the metal door through which the two men had dragged the third. Bolan tried the handle.

Locked. He began to formulate his next move when he heard the sound of one of the bay doors rising. Bolan sprinted along the dock and reached the bay door directly behind the truck trailer when it was about halfway up. He put his back to the wall, trying desperately to become a part of it, hoping that his form wouldn't be noticeable. If nothing else, he had to keep his presence quiet as long as possible until he could verify the target.

Two men, different from the men Bolan had seen before, suddenly emerged from the bay doorway. They didn't notice him, their entire focus apparently directed toward the truck. One of the men mumbled something in Spanish—fished out a cigarette and lit it—while the second man went about removing the padlock from the rear door. Together, the men raised the door and stepped into the interior. Bolan saw his chance and took it, rushing the pair and extending his arms straight out to his sides. He struck them full force, knocking the men into the truck, which was only half-filled with large crates. Before the men could recover, Bolan jumped into the air and snagged the heavy cord hanging from the door. It landed home with a slam and Bolan immediately secured it with the padlock one of the men had casually tossed aside on the dock.

Bolan whirled and proceeded inside the bay, looking around in all directions before locating the two-button switch and lowering the bay door. Whatever it was the men had intended to unload, it would take them some time. Bolan was betting nobody would be looking for them to return soon. That meant there were at least two more still inside, the ones who had earlier removed and dragged the unconscious driver into the massive building. With luck, Bolan would be able to find the meth-processing facility inside the structure before he encountered them again.

The Executioner brought his Beretta into play again and proceeded deeper into the bowels of the factory.

10

"That's it, man," Rumaldo Salto announced. "I think Hector's lost his mind."

"Hey, home slice, you best not say that too loud," Rico Cazuela, one of Salto's crewmembers, replied. Cazuela had always been a kiss-ass but he was as loyal as they came. A former courier like Salto, Cazuela's recruitment into their very closed organization had been personally approved by Casco. Casco believed in treating his people like family once they proved themselves. That's something Salto couldn't fault him for, and he maintained his loyalty for that reason alone. Cazuela added, "Hector hears you talking like that, he's likely to cut off your balls with a dull knife."

"That's for sure," Ricky Preciado added. "The boss's never been a guy who puts up with somebody questioning his orders. He tells you to do something and you do it, otherwise you're likely to end up in the grave."

Preciado wasn't any different than Cazuela, except maybe he was a bit smarter. Preciado had been educated in one of the finest schools in Mexico City. There were few people working for Casco who could say that, Salto included. In spite of his education, though, Preciado didn't seem all that bright. It was probably one of the reasons Salto had taken the lead position after Casco's last house boss ended up getting drunk and mouthing off to a member of Los Zetas. Still, it was Salto's job to keep things under control and carry out Casco's instructions to the letter, whether he agreed with them or not. If Cazuela was right about anything, it was that Casco wouldn't put up with disobedience of any kind. The man viewed doing what you were told as the tourist measure of loyalty—and Salto wasn't about to do something that would make his boss think he wasn't loyal. If he was planning to do that, it would've been better for him to just put the gun to his head and pull the trigger himself.

Still, this plan seemed a little over the top—crazier than anything Casco had ever asked him to do before. Salto had to admit the idea of attempting to kidnap a high-ranking official like the governor was ballsy and nobody could deny it, but that still didn't make it a smart move. Salto had to ask himself if he'd be able to pull it off when the moment came. He hadn't been able to bust a cap on Claudia—he only hoped the stupid bitch understood it would mean both their lives if she ever returned to Phoenix—which made him think that somewhere along the line he'd become squeamish.

A few years ago, nobody would have ever described him that way. When Salto had joined Los Negros, even before he became house boss, he'd acquired a reputation as a tough professional. Had he developed a conscience? Maybe he had, but it wouldn't do him any good to run down the boss or his plan in front of Cazuela and Preciado. He'd never known either of them to repeat anything they discussed, but he couldn't rely on that alone; not when it could mean his very life if one of them decided to go back and repeat what he said to Casco.

"It's fucking hot," Cazuela said.

Salto was actually happy for the change in subject. "We won't have to sit out here much longer. She finished her speech over an hour ago, which means she'll be showing up here in a short time."

"I hope so," Preciado replied. "'Cause if you ask me, we're taking a big risk sitting out here in the middle of the block where everybody can see us."

"Ricky, why don't you take a break?"

For a moment, Preciado looked like he might argue with Salto but one look from the house boss let him know that it was neither a request nor negotiable.

"That's fine," Preciado said. "I could use a smoke anyway."

It worked out for all of them, since Salto absolutely abhorred cigarette smoke and didn't permit it in Casco's house. He also didn't allow any of the sentries to smoke while they were on duty. Especially at night, since he knew from his experience as a courier and a mule that a cigarette cherry could be seen from as far as two hundred yards. Not to mention that an outside observer would be able to see exactly where sentries were positioned based only on the harsh odor of burning tobacco.

Preciado bailed from the car and lit up as he'd made a respectable distance.

One of the things Salto had ordered them to do was to dress in clothes appropriate for the area. This was an exclusive neighborhood, filled with upper-class snobs and rich bitches who took great pride in the fact they lived in this sort of community. They were yuppies, millionaires and self-made types who expected the very best in everything for no other reason than they could afford it. It had surprised Salto when Casco told him that the governor lived in such a neighborhood. Okay, so Arizona didn't maintain a mansion for the state's top whore; that didn't come as a real surprise to him. What did come as a surprise was that she didn't live in a gated community, or a place where at least there was security.

"Hey, we got something here, boss," Cazuela said.

He started to reach for the ignition but Salto grabbed his hand. "Just wait a minute. Settle your ass down, we don't want to spook them. We need to handle this exactly the way the boss told us to, otherwise we might blow it."

"What about Ricky?"

"Call his cell and tell him to get his ass back here."

Cazuela did as instructed while Salto monitored the big, black Lincoln Town Car that rolled past their vehicle. Salto had ordered them to keep their windows up, allowing them to remain open just a hair. This had built a stifling heat inside the vehicle but Salto couldn't risk someone spotting them. The window tint was dark enough to keep them from being observed by outsiders. Under normal circumstances, such a dark tint wasn't permitted by law but the Phoenix police had better things to do. In fact, it was the local gangs who had provided many of those distractions that Los Negros used to their advantage.

Basically, it came down to the fact that the cops were so busy busting petty criminals in the local gangs, they didn't have the resources to go after groups like Los Negros and Los Zetas. This had allowed Casco and his competitors to operate with significant impunity, turning up the heat on each other wherever and whenever it was necessary. It seemed almost too easy when Salto considered it, going up against a bunch of young punks who thought because they could rip off an old lady's purse or paint gang signs on the wall that suddenly they were the real shit.

Oh, well, Salto had been there once himself, and he could have told any one of those juvenile delinquents they didn't know what it meant to be the real shit.

But none of it made a difference at this moment. Salto and his crew had one objective, the woman named Elizabeth Kampp. She had become a priceless artifact in Casco's war against the cops, against the man they called the Devil in Black and against Los Zetas—the very group run like men not unlike his boss, whose only motive was to seek his complete and utter destruction. Failure wasn't an option, and whether

Salto agreed with Casco or not, he would not be labeled as unfaithful or disloyal.

One way or another, Elizabeth Kampp would become his prize today.

"I THOUGHT YOUR SPEECH was very good, Governor," Beau Hastings said as they rode toward Kampp's palatial home.

Normally, Hastings would not have accompanied her back to the house but Kampp felt so sorry for him after all he had revealed earlier—his most secret fears and worries—that she invited him to a quiet dinner with her family.

Kampp smiled graciously. "Thank you, Beau."

For some reason she couldn't explain, the silence weighed heavy between them and she wasn't even sure why. It wasn't as if they'd ever had difficulty carrying on a conversation before, even small talk. She wondered if perhaps Hastings perceived he'd crossed the line with her during that uncomfortable moment in her office. She had to admit that it had made her a little uneasy, as well, but she understood that Hastings was a private man and for him to reveal such things had taken great courage.

Kampp had always admired men of courage, irrespective of their political or social views. Hastings also possessed a number of very noble traits. He was loyal, efficient and every bit as loving and caring about other people as he was himself. Kampp had to admit that her life and politics had jaded her view of people in general. She had learned to mistrust others, particularly their motives, and she saw most of them as opportunists. Then again, the governor had to lend some credence to the idea that her feelings stemmed solely from those with whom she had surrounded herself.

If anyone had suggested to her almost fifteen years ago—when she had first entered state politics as a wide-eyed and ambitious young woman with a law degree so fresh the ink hadn't even dried on the diploma—that the people she would eventually call friends and allies were actually some of the most vile and disgusting members of the human race, Kampp would've laughed in their face. Over time she learned to accept it was nothing more than the unmitigated truth, although she had way too much class to tell people who were just starting out about the things that she'd learned. Whenever she went and campaigned or gave speeches, and young people came up to her and told her how she inspired them, Kampp would simply smile and encourage them to pursue whatever their interests might be in the political arena.

Inside, the fact that she would not take the time to build courage enough to tell them to look for a more rewarding career crushed her spirits. She wanted to grab them by the shoulders, to shake some sense into them, but she just couldn't bring herself to do it. The fact that she would not tell them about the regrets that she had of entering politics, not reveal to them all of the dirty little secrets she knew from spending so many years around the worst of the worst, made her feel like a fraud. That's why she could admire men like Hastings.

The Lincoln Town Car turned the corner and proceeded up the street toward the double gates marking the entrance to the Kampp property. Several of the motorcycle unit police officers had been detailed by the chief of police to accompany her to her home. The governor had dissuaded them from following her, indicating that would probably draw more attention than if she were to skip the customary motorcade. The chief of police had seemed hesitant at first, almost as if he wanted to argue with her, but he knew better and his career knew better.

Kampp glanced only briefly at a dark, late-model BMW with tinted windows parked at the curb. She couldn't see inside but Kampp didn't remember having seen the vehicle before. She heard they would be getting new neighbors soon, a young couple who had purchased the house just down the street from their own residence. The place was an older-model Victorian, very unusual architecture for this area, but no less beautiful and so the residents hadn't complained about it bringing down their property values. Besides, like most of the houses in this area, the place was set far off the main street behind walls covered with creeping vines and other niceties. At least, there were niceties around here.

One of the things that Kampp had tried to improve was the water situation in the city. There might have been a lot of money in Phoenix and the surrounding areas—no big surprise given that the large majority of residents were not year-rounders and that Phoenix was the hot spot as a retirement community—but that didn't mean they had to treat Phoenix like a desert Cadillac. There were more residences in the city alone in violation of water conservation than most of the Sun City's suburbia and it frustrated Kampp to no end.

"Are you hungry?" Kampp asked Hastings.

Her young aide patted his stomach in a fashion that would have seemed in place only in a Dickens novel. "I am absolutely ravenous. I cannot wait to see what José has in store for us tonight."

"I'm sure it will be fabulous," Kampp replied. "As always."

"He simply *must* give me his recipe for the bread pudding we had last Christmas. I coaxed him in every way I knew possible up to and including bribery, but he would not budge. I'm hoping he'll be more amenable to the suggestion this year, and will perhaps let some little tidbit slip."

Kampp could only laugh at this. "You know, Beau, there are some days where you can be nothing short of an absolute cad."

"You ought to see me on my really good days," Hastings said as he crossed his legs, folded his hands neatly over his knee and batted his eyelashes.

This only brought another session of uproarious laughter from Kampp. There were days when Hastings could be absolutely hysterical, a one-man show of humor that seemed perfectly natural on him, but would have been out of place on just about anybody else. Hastings had the ability to be humorous without even trying, and it was that spontaneous wit of his that Kampp admired. He could even get the rest of her family laughing, Henry included, without having to try hard. There were times when Kampp wanted to simply throw her arms around him, to tell him how much she valued their friendship and his support.

It was moments like these that made it all worth it.

"Governor Kampp?"

The voice of their driver suddenly drilled through her laughter like a hot poker through an ice block.

Kampp hadn't known this new guy for long. His name was Marcus…Marcus, oh, for Pete's sake, she couldn't even remember his last name. He'd been selected by Hastings as a replacement for their last driver, who had, of all things, won the state lottery and upon learning that he held the winning ticket, walked into Hastings's office, dropped the keys on his desk and walked out without a word. Witnesses later reported that the man left the capitol building with a grin so big and broad it nearly knocked people down.

"What is it, Marcus?"

"Um, I think we have a problem, ma'am."

Kampp furrowed her eyebrows. "What do you mean a problem? What kind of problem?"

As Marcus brought the vehicle to a halt, he pointed toward a figure visible through the front windshield. The man wore sunglasses, a neat linen suit and had dark hair. Besides that, nothing about him spelled high society—especially the very deadly-looking pistol he held level and steady in their direction.

Kampp took a sharp breath and for a moment the only thing she could think of was how Henry had insisted she have the Town Car reinforced with special plating in key areas. His concern had been that someone might try to plant a bomb under the vehicle, and when he wouldn't let it go she finally acquiesced. What nobody had thought of, her loving and devoted husband included, was that someone might actually attempt to shoot her or hijack the vehicle. Who would be stupid enough to make such an absurd attempt on the governor of the state of Arizona? All of her protections and all of her staff, the number of police and other emergency personnel at her disposal, had left her with a sense of immunity.

But she had never considered until that very moment her own vulnerability. Armor plating along the undercarriage in the quarter panels would do nothing to stop a hail of automatic weapons fire.

"What are your orders, Governor?" Marcus said.

"Don't do anything rash," she replied.

"Don't do anything rash?" Hastings shouted. "Shouldn't we get out of here?"

Kampp pinned him with a stony gaze, keeping her voice calm and level. "I am not about to do anything that would risk your lives. Whatever these men want, we are going to cooperate with them and we are not going to fight back."

"So much for your speech, Elizabeth," Hastings said. In quick afterthought, he added, "I'm sorry…that was totally out of line and I'm so sorry."

Kampp reached out and gripped his forearm. "I understand, and I don't want you to worry. Nothing is going to happen to us."

Of course, the very words sounded ridiculous to her even as she said them. How did she know nothing would happen to them? She wasn't in control of the situation any more than either of the men accompanying her, and she had to accept the fact that the gun-toting figure might very well be here for no other purpose than to kill her. Anyone who did want to kill her would not likely leave witnesses behind—in which case everything she had just told her loyal friend and aide had been complete bullshit.

"Now, before we do anything else we need to—"

The door opened suddenly on Hastings's side and a second man, this one much bigger but dressed in a very similar fashion to the first, reached in and hauled Hastings out of the vehicle. Her aide began to shout, practically screeching, and hammered on the man's chest with his fists. Kampp tried to warn him, yelling at him to stop, but Hastings's panic had overtaken him and the only thing he could hear at that point was his own fear. The man shoved Hastings backward, attempting to stave off the assault but to no avail.

Kampp shouted once more at Hastings, ordered him to stop fighting, but her words fell on deaf ears. A moment later it didn't matter as she saw the flash of sunlight on metal. Then the man's hand appeared and jabbed Hastings in the stomach, and the young man folded as the knife blade disappeared beneath his shirt. The man stabbed Hastings again, and then a third time, and Kampp could only scream at him to stop. On the fourth plunge of the blade Hastings toppled to the cement at the man's feet. He still moaned as the big guy turned to reach inside for Kampp.

Marcus had witnessed the struggle in the side mirror of the sedan and at the sight of the man turning for Kampp he bolted out the door and laid both hands on the guy's shoulders. A brief staccato of gunfire rang out and Marcus staggered a moment before dropping from view.

Kampp slapped at the big gorilla's hands as he tried to grab her.

"Hold still, bitch!" the man said, muttering Spanish curses under his breath.

Kampp felt herself fall backward as the rear door on her side of the vehicle opened and strong hands grabbed her arms and hauled her violently from the interior into the baking afternoon sun. A hand clamped over her mouth and then she smelled the biting, acrid stench of some kind of chemical. Was it chloroform perhaps, or ether, something as old-fashioned as that? Oddly, she thought about how the only thing missing was a dastardly type in a black hat twirling his handlebar mustache as some evil sidekick tied her to railroad tracks.

Why she would have ever thought of such a silly thing she couldn't understand, but from the moment her captors clamped the rag over her mouth she found herself no longer thinking straight. And then a moment later, she dropped off without any conscious thought at all.

11

It didn't take Bolan long to figure out somebody was following him. He'd only been in the factory for a couple of minutes before realizing he'd picked up the tail.

But what the Executioner couldn't understand is why they were following. Why not just grab him right there; get a team of men together and simply overpower him by sheer numbers? These were professional enforcers for Casco, members of Los Negros who allegedly had been trained to maintain the security of a place like this. How hard could it be? Unless it wasn't a member of security following at all. Bolan could tell that it wasn't a pro on his tail—this was an amateur all the way.

Bolan turned the corner of an area surrounded by tall racks on both sides, the metal kinds assembled with nuts and bolts and reinforced by heavy shelving. A good number of the shelves were devoid of anything resembling Casco's alleged manufacturing business. There were no machine parts, no crates and nothing that would indicate that a prosperous business thrived here. Bolan wondered how Casco had managed to get away with such a structure for this long. He knew that there were regular inspectors who came to ensure that any Mexican nationals working within the factory were doing so under safe conditions. Then again, a guy with Casco's connections could have explained away just about anything, not to mention the fact that some of the inspectors probably had their palms greased repeatedly to keep their mouths shut about any indiscretions they may have found.

And why not?

It was good business for the Mexican government because it put citizens into jobs. People who had money generally weren't taken to committing crimes, and the more Mexican citizens working, the less chance of crime and the less headache for the government. Mexican officials already had their hands full with all of the drug trafficking and gang activities. People were being slaughtered in major border cities left and right, attempts by the more powerful cartels and larger gangs to show that they were still the ones in charge. Such activities might have intimidated others, but they didn't intimidate a man like Bolan. He'd seen that stuff way too many times to let it bother him. At least, it didn't worry him in the way it worried so many others.

When Bolan worried, he worried for the poor bystanders who were often the victims of the criminals. As long as the gangs and cartels were able to turn a profit they didn't much care who died in the process. They had no conscience and no moral or ethical ambitions. The only things they responded to were money and power. Well, Bolan had an alternative response and he didn't much care how major the losses suffered by the enemy would be. He would've taken them in a fight, fair or unfair, and done anything to win. That was the difference between the Executioner and those in the cartels. They fought for money and prestige, but Bolan fought for an ideal.

Through his many exploits against the enemies of freedom and peace, Bolan had often carried the paraphrase from famous author Victor Hugo: "No army is as strong as an idea whose time has come."

As soon as Bolan rounded the corner he dashed up the

aisle, found a shelf with a crate on it and stepped between the edge of the uprights and the crate. He held the Beretta muzzle pointed toward the ceiling of the shelf above his head, crouched in the shadows and waited for the follower to pass his position. He didn't need to wait long. The young boy who walked on by couldn't have been more than twelve or thirteen. He seemed so focused on tracking Bolan he was completely oblivious to the Executioner's hiding place.

There's no way the Mexican inspectors could have let that go by. Child labor for any Mexican citizen under the age of sixteen was strictly forbidden by national law. No American company could enter into a contract with a foreign nation for the procurement or hiring of laborers under the age of sixteen, save for children who signed up within the month of their sixteenth birthday. It appeared that Casco, if he did in fact oversee this factory, didn't mind taking the risk of being caught. But as Kurtzman had pointed out, Casco's name was in no way affiliated with this place except in the most indirect fashion.

Bolan waited a moment, letting the kid make some distance before stepping into view and pursuing his young tail. The hunter had now become the hunted, and Bolan had to wonder for a moment if the kid might have a backup. It was entirely possible he was a child of one of the workers here, maybe one who had been under some sort of day-care program and managed to escape. Bolan could see how such a thing might happen and it didn't really surprise him that much.

The Executioner had nearly overtaken the boy when he heard a series of clangs and bangs, and then what sounded like a conveyor start up. The noises covered Bolan's approach and he seized the advantage to grab the youth and clamp a hand over his mouth. The kid reacted with incredible speed. He nearly squirmed out of Bolan's grasp while simultaneously stomping on the Executioner's instep. Bolan grunted with the impact, however minimal, given that most of the boy's small heel contacted the steel toe and rigid shank protecting the top of Bolan's foot.

Bolan caught a flutter of movement in his peripheral vision as a pair of armed sentries passed into view at the far end of the aisle intersecting where they stood. Bolan scanned the area quickly and spotted an alcove overshadowing a door. He half carried, half dragged the struggling boy to the door, found it unlocked and pushed inside. Bolan eased the door closed with his foot while maintaining a hold of the boy. Once it had closed, Bolan locked it and then released his grip on the kid's mouth.

They stood on the landing of a dimly lit stairwell, the area musty and dirty with disuse—a good sign that they wouldn't be bothered here, at least long enough for him to question the kid.

"Let…me…go!" the kid insisted, attempting to jerk his arm free with every enunciation.

"Quiet," Bolan growled.

"Let me go, or I yell."

Bolan clamped his hand over the kid's mouth again. "You're doing a good job of that now. If I'm discovered here I'm dead, and if you're seen with me you'll end up the same way. You understand *that?*"

The boy's eyes widened, the whites surrounding the dark brown orbs almost luminescent in their dungeonlike confines. Satisfied the kid understood the consequences of any additional outbursts, Bolan removed his hand but maintained a firm grip on the boy's arm. The Executioner might have been empathetic to his plight but he wasn't stupid. This one had already proven to be a little pistol and Bolan couldn't take the chance the kid might actually be on the enemy's side. He would never have harmed the boy but he had no qualms about tying him up, gagging him and stuffing him in a nice dark closet somewhere until he could complete his objectives.

"What's your name?" Bolan asked, figuring it was best to

establish a rapport before the kid had a chance to rethink his position.

The kid was surprisingly forthcoming and very purposeful in his response. "I am Soledad, but I no like that name."

Bolan felt almost ridiculous standing in this dusty stairwell having a halfway serious discussion with this little vagrant who was obviously more troublesome than he appeared with his almost feminine facial features and big brown eyes. His mop of curly hair looked unkempt and unwashed, and the dirt on his arms and face was visible even in the dull glow of the stairwell lights.

"Okay then, what should I call you?" Bolan asked gently.

"I like Duke."

"Duke."

"Yes, I like Duke."

"Okay then," Bolan said. "What are you doing creeping around here...Duke?"

"I suppose to be here. What you doing here, mister?"

That caused Bolan to grin. "That's a pretty long story and one I don't have time to tell right now."

The kid looked a little disappointed. "But I like stories. Like the kind Senora Minoza tell us."

"And who's Senora Minoza?"

"She's our watcher. She watch us during the day while Momma works."

"Where does your mom work?" Bolan asked. "Here in the factory?"

The boy nodded with an enthusiastic grin that included a missing front tooth. The kid might have been a little dirty but he looked healthy and well-nourished; a bit of a surprise given the economy and the water filtration systems in this part of the country. Bolan wondered for a moment if they had him doing some kind of work because his hands seemed particularly dirty and rough, much rougher than those he would've expected on a child his age.

"Do you work here, too?"

He shook his head. "I'm no allowed to work yet. But soon, real soon, I'll be able to work. Senora Minoza says I'm best and will do a good job."

Now Bolan felt a burning sensation in his gut, and his face reddened. It took on such a dangerous hue, in fact, that Duke's expression transformed from exuberant to almost plaintive and he stepped back a respectful distance. Bolan didn't mean to scare the little guy but Duke's statement confirmed the Executioner's worst suspicions. They were using these kids for some type of labor and if it were legitimate work he might have let it slide, but if they were using them around a factory secretly producing meth, then Bolan meant to deal with that. Immediately.

A sudden rattle of the door handle quelled any further exchange between them. Bolan put his finger to his lips and then gestured for the boy to get up the stairs. He hadn't planned to go up but this mischievous kid had thrown a bit of a monkey wrench into the works, and Bolan felt responsible for his wellbeing. He couldn't let his new little friend get hurt.

Bolan mounted the steps two at a time and when Duke started to slow him down he scooped the boy into his arms and continued vaulting the stairwell. They reached the secondfloor landing and Bolan could hear an incessant pounding on the metal door, the steady thumps echoing up the dingy confines. Bolan discarded his human burden at the top of the stairs and silenced him with a hand.

Duke grinned broadly but kept his peace.

Bolan opened the door and peered into a long hallway. The hall had a series of doors, most likely the administrative offices, but at the moment it was devoid of foot traffic. Bolan could barely detect voices due to the incessant pounding below. That didn't bother the Executioner nearly as much as the fact that the place was lit up like a baseball stadium. There wouldn't be any way for him to move down the hallway without being seen, so he would have to rely on speed and stealth to get him through undetected.

Bolan turned and looked at Duke. "Okay, pal, I'm only going to say this once. We're going to walk down that hallway and we're not going to make a sound."

"Why we have to be quiet?" Duke demanded.

"I've already explained that. You've seen the men who walk around here with guns?"

Duke just nodded.

"Those men are very bad men, men who won't think one moment about hurting me or you. And if they can't get near you, then they might just try to get to your mom. I don't want anything to happen to you and I don't want anything to happen to her. So if you can help me get to where I need to go, then I promise that I'll make sure that you and your mom get out of here safe. Is that a deal?"

Duke appeared to give it serious thought, and then stuck his hands in the pockets of his filthy jeans and smiled. His dark eyes had taken on a shifty quality, the kind one only saw in the eyes of some bartering trinket vendor on the street of a backwater, third world country.

"I help you," he said. "For ten dollar, U.S."

"How about you do it for free because we're friends?"

"I no sure you're my friend." Duke held out his hand. "You give me ten dollar, U.S., I'd be quiet and take you where you want to go."

The Executioner considered alternatives and realized he didn't really have any. For some strange reason, this little urchin had decided to latch on to him, and obviously figured Bolan—a tall American who had gotten himself in over his head—would be desperate enough to pay the little business-man some *dinero* and not turn him over to the mean guys with machine guns. The entire situation bordered so close to ridiculous that Bolan almost had to laugh. But in reality, the soldier knew he didn't have much of a choice if he wanted to get out of there alive.

Bolan sighed and reached into his pocket. He always kept a small roll of cash on hand just in case he needed it. Bolan had walked on most every continent, in nearly every country, and he couldn't remember a moment where he had been robbed so blindly by such innocence. This was definitely one of those times in his career where he would be able to tell the interesting story of a little Mexican boy named Soledad, who actually preferred to be called Duke.

"Okay, little man," Bolan said as he peeled two twenty-dollar bills from his stash. "Here's forty dollars, U.S., cold hard cash."

Duke's eyes lit up and as he reached for it Bolan pulled it back and looked at him with a serious expression. "Now this is four times what you asked for. There isn't going to be any more, so don't bother trying to bribe me again. We got a deal?"

Duke snatched the money in his pocket and stuck out his hand. "We got a deal, mister."

Bolan shook the young boy's hand and then turned to the door as he drew his Beretta. He eased the door open, took one more look in both directions and slipped into the hallway with the little opportunist named Duke in tow. They nearly made it to the end of the hall when the sound of the door opening behind them caught Bolan's attention. The Executioner turned in time to see a uniformed security officer emerge from a side door. In other circumstances, Bolan might have sought cover in one of the offices before they were spotted, but in this case there was absolutely nowhere they could disappear fast enough.

Not that it mattered, since the man who stepped into the hallway—despite the professional-looking uniform that he wore—was in no way an example of legitimate security. First off, his hair was pulled straight back into a massive ponytail that then wrapped itself back over his right shoulder and was tied off with a cord from which three miniature skulls made of pewter hung. There were red stones of some kind in the eyelets of the skulls. Along his left forearm was a tattoo, one Bolan recognized from the intelligence files he'd studied prior to his arrival in Phoenix. The man wore the mark of a hitter for none other than Los Negros. There was little doubt in Bolan's mind he was looking at one of Casco's goons.

The guy clawed for hardware on his hip the moment he spotted Bolan, but the Executioner was already in motion. Bolan raised the Beretta as he shoved his young ward to the thin carpet and stepped just forward to shield the boy's body with his own massive form. At the same moment as the enemy gunman cleared his pistol from leather, Bolan snap-aimed and squeezed the trigger twice. The first 9 mm Parabellum round traveled the distance in under a second and opened a third hole in the man's nose. His head snapped backward as the bullet flattened, crunching bone and ripping through brain matter before lodging in the base of his skull. The second round was mere insurance, entering through the left side of his chest and punching a hole in his heart. The enemy's body hit the floor about the same time as Bolan hauled Duke to his feet and steered him toward the exit.

It didn't surprise Bolan to hear a wail of fright escape from Duke's lips as they rushed for the door. What he was taken aback by was the youngster's blubbering apologies for not being quiet, and begging Bolan not to take his money back. Duke's fear nearly broke Bolan's heart as he thought about how few of the good things in life Duke had probably known. For all Bolan knew, the little guy didn't even have a father around.

When they reached the exit, Bolan could hear the excited shouts of a few of the braver ones who had come out of their offices to investigate the commotion. Although Bolan had chambered the pistol with subsonic cartridges, it still made enough noise in the narrow hallway to draw attention. It was the kind of attention Bolan didn't need, especially since he wasn't anywhere close to finding the meth-processing facility that he was now certain *had* to be somewhere on the grounds.

As they descended in a freight elevator that Bolan had discovered once they were away from the offices, he wondered for a moment if Duke might not know where it was located. It would save them some time, but he could no longer guarantee Duke's safety or that of his mother's. No, he wouldn't put the kid at any more risk than he already had; he would have to find another way.

"You want me show you what bad guys do?"

Bolan looked down at Duke, the shaky voice breaking him from his thoughts. "What did you say?"

"You want to know what bad guys do?"

As Bolan stared a moment, trying to figure out what Duke was offering, the little boy sniffed and rubbed at his eyes where the tears had stained his dirty face to reveal something resembling clean skin beneath them.

"Are you saying you know what those men are doing here?"

The young boy nodded. "My brother tell me, because he know I'm going to do the same as him one day. That's what Senora Minoa tell me I so good at. That one day I can do like my brother, and take the product they make across to America. I go to America some day."

The fury burned in Bolan's gut. They were training this young, impressionable boy to be a mule. They were training him to haul drugs across the border so they could distribute their high-priced death to the schools and homes of Americans too tempted by quick cash and a quicker high to know or care what was really happening. Not that it would have necessarily changed anything. Nonetheless, it incensed Bolan and only steeled his resolve to destroy this death house once and for all.

"Yes," he replied quietly. "Yes, Duke. Show me what the bad men are doing."

12

Captain Joseph Hall stared at the horrific scene before him.

Detectives, state police, the office of the state medical examiner and a war of criminal forensics specialists and technicians buzzed around him, but he hardly took notice of their activities. Black tarps covered the bodies of two of Governor Elizabeth Kampp's closest staff. Hall and his team had been out preparing to conduct their sixth raid of the day when the call came over the radio car channel. Dispatchers were advising that shots had been fired in the region of the governor's residence, and all available units were asked to respond to a code three.

Hall's unit had been the first to arrive, and after ordering his men to secure the scene he approached the point of the carnage. Two bodies, one of whom they had identified as Marcus Simpson, and the other as Beau Hastings—the governor's driver/bodyguard and senior aide respectively—lay in front of Kampp's Lincoln Town Car in a pool of congealed blood. Governor Elizabeth Kampp was nowhere to be found, and three of the four car doors were still open. Nobody had seen anything and the shots-fired call had actually come from the house on the next block over.

"This is some seriously fucked-up shit," Sergeant Larry

Murach said under his breath as he joined Hall's brooding vigil.

"You kidding me?" Hall snapped. "It's a hell of a lot more than that, Larry. In just a short time we're going to have an army of goddamned federal agents crawling all over this place. Our friend Brognola in Washington agreed to get a crew here at the request of the governor. Now she's out there somewhere, but it's anybody's guess whether she's still alive or not, and we're sitting here with our thumbs up our asses waiting for some support that may or may not come anytime soon.

"And you know what sticks in my craw more than anything else? Huh? It's that not two hours ago, Kampp stood up in front of an army of press and told them that the citizens of Phoenix no longer have any reason to worry because, and I quote her here, 'I can say with much confidence that we will have a resolution to this issue in a very short time. Thanks to the President of the United States and the FBI, Captain Hall and his flying squad of specialized police officers will have virtually unlimited resources with which to combat this problem.' Yeah, oh, yeah, that's what she said to the press. That would be the same press that's now standing on the other side of the yellow tape, who I'm sure have a lot of questions on how we, who are supposed to be getting all this federal support, could now let the governor of the state of Arizona be snatched up by these cocksuckers while we stand around in a circle waiting for somebody to make some decent goddamned decisions around here."

Murach admitted by expression alone, eyes wide and jaw slack, that he didn't have any answer for that. That was the most difficult thing for the policeman to accept. The crooks had just taken the governor out from under their noses, and there wasn't one damn thing he could do about it. He had no leads and no idea where to start looking. Well, this was something they couldn't just let go. Even if he let the state police take over, waited for the FBI support to arrive, they wouldn't have any more answers than he did.

"It's that damned Brognola cat that got us into this," Hall spat as he wheeled in place and stepped smartly in the direction of the tactical van. "And he's damn well going to get us out of this."

Once they were inside, Hall ordered Murach to round up the rest of the men to assist the uniforms in a canvas. After Murach left, Hall asked the technicians inside to take a break so he could have some privacy. When he was alone, Hall donned a phone headset and dialed the number that Cooper had given him that was supposedly a direct line to the man called Harold Brognola. Brognola picked up the phone on the first ring, and Hall immediately recognized his voice.

"Mr. Brognola, this is Captain Joe Hall with the Phoenix Police Department."

"I've been expecting your call," Brognola said.

"Is that right? Well that's good, then you must know why it is I'm calling."

"We're already aware the governor has been kidnapped. I can assure you we're taking every necessary action even as we speak. I've been authorized to plug the dam here, and I can promise that you will have our complete support. There's an inbound flight to Phoenix right now with a dozen federal agents and a couple of the top kidnapping experts in the country. They should be setting down at the airport within the hour."

"Well I hope there's a clairvoyant among them," Hall barked. "Because I'm here to tell you that's what it's going to take to find Governor Kampp."

"Captain Hall, I realize that this is a difficult time for you and I understand the frustrations you've been experiencing. But up until this point, you've not had the kind of support that we're providing you. You have also not had the kind of results since we began to provide that support, so I think that it's not unconscionable that we would ask you for a little bit of latitude while we deal with the situation."

"Deal with the situation? I don't mean to seem ungrateful here, Brognola, because I know that you must come from a pretty significant law enforcement background."

"How would you know that?"

"You're kidding. Right?" Hall let out a chuckle. "I've been a cop for the better part of fifteen years, pal. I know when I'm talking to another cop. At least, I suspect you used to be one and I'm hoping and praying you haven't become another Washington bureaucrat."

"Oh, you can bet that nobody who knows me will tell you I'm a bureaucrat. I'm anything but, and I'd be willing to guess that you and I have many of the same views about what it takes to get results. In fact, at this very moment I can tell you that Cooper's running down a factory just over the border in Nogales. We've been led to understand that it's one of the major meth production facilities that Hector Casco has under his thumb."

"So you're trying to tell me that piece of shit has the balls to produce meth under the noses of the Mexican government, and then turns around and mules the stuff across the border under the noses of our own people?"

"I don't know if I'd put it that dramatically," Brognola replied, "but I would say you've pretty much got the picture, yeah."

"Well if Casco is too busy trying to protect his interests in this area, what reason does he have to kidnap the governor?"

"I'm not suggesting that you're incorrect about who's behind her kidnapping, but I'd be interested to hear your thoughts on why you think that it's Hector Casco who's taken Governor Kampp. What makes you think it's not Jorge Cárdonas?"

"Who?"

"Jorge Cárdonas is Casco's alter ego in the Gulf cartel.

We have reason to believe that Casco's made contact with Cárdonas, probably because they've realized that it wasn't Los Zetas or any of Cárdonas's people that hit Casco's lieutenants at their club. Cooper is convinced that Casco is well aware of his presence, and he figured the only way he could put a damper on their activities was to give them a unified target. He's hitting Casco's factory so that he can draw them away from what's happening in Phoenix and give you an opportunity to work."

"Let's say you're right about that. That leaves little doubt to Casco as our first, most logical choice in this kidnapping."

"Okay," Brognola said. "So I ask again what makes you think so?"

"Well, it's obvious Casco doesn't want to lose control of the situation here. He figures if he loses the buy-in here and now, he'll never be able to regain a foothold in this territory. Not only will that cause this kidnapping ring to collapse, it'll also destabilize his position with his own people and the competitors. He figures the only way he can stop us from hitting them hard and heavy is a distraction. Kidnapping the governor of this state would definitely get the job done."

"Well, I'll be damned," Brognola said with a booming laugh. "Don't look now, but you're starting to sound an awful lot like Cooper."

"No reason to get personal," Hall quipped.

"All right, I'll tell you what I'm going to do. Let me run this by some resources here and see what we can come up with. Maybe we can get you pointed in the right direction. That seem fair enough?"

"Do I have a choice, Brognola?"

"No, not really. I'll be in touch."

The connection clicked off and left only dead air in its wake. Hall pulled the telephone headset from his ear, looked at it a moment and then muttered a curse before dropping it on a nearby field table and stomping out of the mobile command center.

"I HAVE TO ADMIT, I like the way this Joe Hall thinks," Brognola announced.

Price wrapped her long, elegant fingers around a stack of paperwork and dropped it gently on the lit glass tabletop in the briefing room adjacent to the operations center of the annex.

Built a number of years before as an expansion to the original Farmhouse, the Annex was a massive complex built beneath a tree farm and wood-chipping facility used to disguise the true nature of its purpose. Not only did the aboveground building boast a retractable roof, beneath which was housed an antiaircraft missile battery, but the entire complex itself could also remain self-sustaining for months and possibly years given its independent power and water splice.

The various sections of the Annex were separated into a large base, all attached to one another and linked to the original Farmhouse by a thousand-foot tunnel. The Annex was split into the Computer Room, the Communications Center and the Security Operations Center. Massive screens lined many of the walls, and the outermost portions of the Computer Center included offices, storage space and even studio-style living quarters for particularly long and intense missions.

Under some immortal sense of nostalgia, briefings were still conducted in the War Room beneath the Farmhouse. Brognola and Price also choose to maintain their offices in that location, predominantly because there were more comfortable living facilities in the original two-story building. The Farmhouse also had recreational areas, full kitchen amenities and comfortable quarters for Able Team and Phoenix Force members when they were in the rear. Of course, their rooms didn't see much use since they spent most of their time on missions, but it gave them a warm, comfortable and peaceful atmosphere to which they could return and unwind from the stresses of combat.

"What did he give you?" Price said.

"Nothing that we hadn't already thought of but I saw no point in bringing up that part," Brognola replied. "I just appreciate the fact the guy uses his head instead of flying off the handle at the first sign of trouble. This country can always use more police officers like that. I can tell this guy gives a damn. He really cares, like Striker cares."

"Sounds like he has impressed you," Price said with a smile and a wink.

Brognola cleared his throat. "Okay, so let's move on to the more serious matter of Governor Kampp. What do we know?"

"As soon as word came over the wire that she'd been snatched, I asked Bear to start looking into any and all likely places where Casco might have her taken."

"And?"

"The answer actually came from a scrap of information that we found in an old DEA report. However, I'm going to have to bore you with the full history. You'll recall the mission we sent Striker on sometime back that started in Brownsville, Texas. At that time the largest and most powerful Mexican drug cartel was being run by José 'Panchos' Carillo."

Brognola nodded. "Who could forget that? The guy subverted every other major cartel through a campaign of betrayal and murder, and then allied himself with Colonel Nievas of the FARC to supply his drug-smuggling operations with security."

"Right. That was right at the same time that the Kung Lok Chinese triad out of Canada tried to take over the porn and drug operations in Las Vegas, establishing a hold from which they could branch out."

"It almost resulted in a cartel-triad war with the battleground being American streets."

"Well, after Striker brought Carillo down, it became a free-for-all at the border. Of course, the DEA and Border Patrol responded with incredible efficiency. But the tide of illegals coming over the border began to take a priority, and unfortunately the administration at the time started funneling money into social programs to try to educate Mexican nationals so they could reintegrate them into their own culture."

"It was probably one of the largest mistakes we ever made in our foreign policy," Brognola said. "Instead of combating the drug trade, we ended up being a babysitting service for the Mexican government because they could not keep their own border under control."

"You got it," Prince said. "Our lack of diligence ended up giving rise to the Sinaloa and Gulf cartels. It was only a matter of time before they would start to fight each other for control of the Mexican-American drug trade. The Gulf cartel ended up declaring victory down in Ciudad Juárez and El Paso."

"And that's about the same time that the number of kidnappings and drug-related offenses began to rise in Phoenix and the surrounding areas," Brognola concluded. "As usual, Striker was on top of it and he figured there had to be a relationship between the two."

Price sat back and folded her arms, nodding emphatically at Brognola's observation. "The sad thing is that we didn't see it, and yet for Striker it was a foregone conclusion. I'd have to say we dropped the ball on this one, Hal. We should've seen this coming and been in front of it when we had the chance."

"Don't do it, Barb."

"Don't do what?"

"Don't beat yourself up just because you didn't catch it." Brognola stretched, absently inspecting the rumpled suit that he'd been wearing so long now it was beginning to look like he'd slept in it. "I've been doing this a very long time and if there's anything I've learned, it's that you're not going to catch the big fish every time. Unfortunately, we can't have eyes and ears everywhere all the time. These kinds of things will sneak up on you, that's just the nature of the business, and if you let it drive you crazy you *really* become ineffective."

"Okay, fair enough. Is school out now?"

Brognola shrugged, not taking her seriously. He learned after many years of working with Price that she had a dry but charming sense of humor, and one that took some getting used to. Many had wrongly assumed that she was cold and unfeeling, but Brognola knew a much different person lay beneath the thin facade of a calculating professional. Price had no political or personal motives, neither did she take her duties as Stony Man's mission controller lightly.

"Here ends the lesson," Brognola finally said with a chuckle. "So what exactly did this intelligence from the DEA tell us?"

"It seems that once Casco got a foothold in Phoenix, he started undercutting his competitors as well as his allies. This didn't make him particularly popular with the head of the Sinaloa cartel. Apparently, the people he undercut had been fairly good earners in some of the tougher markets. Once Casco had eliminated all of his competition, he started raising prices and his popularity continued to decrease. Finally, a member of the DEA, who ultimately got Gagliardi inside of Casco's operation, had previously inserted an agent who ended up getting killed."

Price turned to a nearby computer terminal that displayed a map of the border between Mexico and Arizona. "I asked Bear to put this together for me so we could send it along to Jack, and he in turn can pass it to Striker. Apparently, Casco decided that if the heat ever got too bad he might have to simply disappear. There's an area about twelve miles northwest of Nogales that is quite rugged and mountainous. According to the intelligence from the DEA, Casco took a good number of his profits and put them into building a fortified estate in this area." A red circle appeared on the screen, a pointer to the general location Price had indicated. "We believe that if Casco is behind the kidnapping of Elizabeth Kampp, this is the most likely place he will take her. Our intelligence suggests it could be well-guarded, extremely difficult to access and virtually impossible to spot from the air."

Of course, it being difficult to spot was no more an issue for the Stony Man teams than it would have been if Casco had painted a large bull's-eye around the hidden base. The electronic surveillance equipment aboard the plane that Jack Grimaldi piloted at this moment toward his rendezvous with Bolan was capable of uncovering such things with relative ease. There were sophisticated infrared systems, communication frequency monitoring devices and a host of other sensitive counterintelligence tools at Grimaldi's disposal.

No, if they had a general area there would be very little chance Grimaldi wouldn't be able to pinpoint the exact location of Casco's hidden firebase. Once they knew that, the Executioner would come up with a plan to get inside the location and rescue Governor Kampp.

"It's safe to assume you've already sent this information to Jack?" Brognola asked.

"Already uploaded to the wireless tactical computer aboard the plane," Price replied. "We also contacted him by phone and apprised him of the current situation. Apparently, he wasn't very far out from the airport, so it's a good bet he's already touched down safely and is waiting for Striker to arrive."

"I hope we're on the money about this one," Brognola said. "I've given my word that we would help the governor squash this thing from the inside out. And now it seems we've been unable to keep the enemy from taking our strongest supporter."

"Remember what you told me just a little bit ago?" Price said. "You know, about how we can't control the fate of the whole world? Don't drive yourself crazy, Hal."

Brognola laughed. "Spoon-feeding me my own medicine, are you? Well, I suppose I had that coming."

"You most definitely did, but you know I only mean it in the nicest sense."

"You know, it's actually ironic."

"What's that?" Price asked, cocking her head.

"When I talked to Governor Kampp, she didn't seem too enthused about giving Striker a chance to deal with the situation. Now it would seem that he's become her first and best hope of getting out of this predicament alive. I wonder what she would say if she knew that?"

"I didn't talk to her, so I can't be sure. But let's hope and pray that in a very short while you'll be able to ask her that yourself."

"Hope and pray I can do," Brognola whispered.

13

True to his word, Duke led Bolan straight to a part of the factory protected by a heavy steel door that slid on a track system powered by hydraulics.

Every moment of their journey, Bolan had to move with stealth and avoid the increased patrols. They hadn't sent out any sort of audible alarm but the Executioner knew they had gone to a full-alert status. There wasn't any way in hell they would let him skip out of there that easily. Bolan had already figured on something like this happening, although having Duke tag along had seriously compromised his mission objectives.

But what could he do?

Leaving the kid behind wasn't a good idea. Witnesses on the second floor, office workers and others, had seen him with Bolan and not being present with the woman Duke called Senora Minoza would have effectively eliminated any alibi he might have. They would only assume he'd helped Bolan in some way—especially if Duke wasn't particularly forthcoming on the details. They would most likely resort to beating the information out of him or taking it out on Duke's mother. That didn't even begin to account for the fact that he'd made a promise to keep the kid and his mother safe, and Bolan was a man of his word.

"Okay, good work," he told the youngster as they lay beneath a conveyor assembly, obscured by the grid work frame that lined either side of it.

"I can take it from here, Duke. But I'm going to need your help. Do you know how to get to your mother?"

Duke nodded emphatically.

"Good," Bolan said, not comforted that much but feeling a little more confident he might just be able to pull it off. "Can you get her away from the bad men, and if you can, is there some place you can hide?"

"I know all the best hiding," Duke said.

For a kid raised in Mexico, Duke's command of the English language impressed Bolan. He probably wasn't formally educated in any way, which meant he'd either learned a large part of what he knew from just listening or he'd watched a lot of television. Based on the moniker he'd chosen for himself, Bolan had to guess that the latter was the more likely story. There were few little boys, American or otherwise, who could resist the adventure pictures featuring the great John Wayne. The character epitomized everything that manhood was supposed to be for a great many youth, and Soledad, aka Duke, had been no exception.

A harsh voice barking what sounded like orders in Spanish distracted Bolan. He tried to listen, pick out critical parts of the conversation, but to no avail.

"You understand what that man's saying?" Bolan asked.

Duke nodded. "He tell the other men to help look for you. He say that I'm with you. They *know* we friends."

"I don't want you to be afraid," Bolan said. "I need for you to be brave and find your mother. Do you know how to get to the docks?"

"*Qué?* What is docks?"

"The docks. The big doors where they park the trucks."

"Ah, *sí*. I know this."

Bolan thought on it another second and then made his decision. "There's a truck parked out there. A big truck like you see comes now and then. You find your mother and take her to that truck, and wait for me there."

"Where you go, mister? I thought we are amigos?"

Bolan rested a hand on the young boy's shoulder. "We are amigos, Duke. But this is important and I have to do this. These men are doing very bad things in my country, in America, and I have to stop them. Otherwise you will have to go into the business your brother is in."

"But I no mind."

"You will when you get older and understand. Maybe someday I'll explain it to you, but for the moment you must do as I ask. Please."

Duke nodded with the callow and characteristic exuberance that comes from youth and a very innocent view toward life. Duke was a boy who knew nothing of corruption. He simply did his thing and if it fit into what others were doing, great. If not, he'd do his own thing anyway and throw caution to the wind. And why not? Duke saw himself as just another John Wayne, and he wasn't dissuaded from something simply because he might not be able to do it.

And Bolan admired the hell out of the kid for that.

"All right then, get moving."

Duke stuck out his hand and when Bolan went to shake it, the boy slapped his palm. He then produced one last grin before scampering out of view, gone so fast Bolan could barely believe it. The kid had definite speed, the soldier had to give him that much.

The Executioner then turned his attention to the matter at hand. The leader who had sent his two men off on a wild-goose chase had made the mistake of staying behind to man their post. The man stood maybe five foot six, weighed all of a buck-fifty soaking wet and didn't appear to be in relatively good shape. It was just that kind of assessment that made Bolan consider how to make his approach. Things usually got dangerous when a soldier started to make assumptions about his enemy.

Bolan decided the only logical approach would be hard and fast, and without ceremony he burst from the concealment as the man turned his back toward the door and charged him like a rushing bull. Bolan made contact before the guy had time to react, shoving him at a point just below his neck and vertically centered beneath the shoulder blades. Simultaneously, the Executioner slipped a foot in front of the man's legs and then kicked back at the last second. The move, known as a trip-hammer technique, facilitated the bashing of the leader's face into the steel door. He slid to the floor, leaving a gory streak in his wake.

Bolan inspected the door, noticed a keycard access system similar to the one he'd seen on the external doors and then frisked the unconscious enemy until he found a swipe card. Bolan extracted the card and passed it through the reader. At first, nothing happened and he experienced a moment of concern. Suddenly, though, the door began to creak and with the clang of a latch it slid open at a turtle's pace.

Bolan had substituted his Beretta for the FNC and when he stepped into the room, he experienced marked gladness for his preparation. A pair of Los Negros commandos whirled and looked him in the eyes before bringing their weapons to bear. Bolan continued his forward movement and made a beeline toward nearby cover as the pair opened up on him with a full salvo. The Executioner rolled the last few feet and came to one knee on the far side of a stack of fifty-five-gallon drums. He leveled the muzzle of the FNC and triggered a short burst that didn't contact either enemy target, but sure made them rethink the fact that they were completely exposed to enemy fire.

One of the pair reacted with admirable skill and found

cover, but the other apparently felt that continuing to pummel Bolan's position with a storm of murderous lead would be all the protection he needed. To a lesser combatant, his idea might have worked. Bolan was hardly a novice, however, and he got the guy by shifting positions out of the line of fire and putting himself in perfect range long enough to get off one more try. The Executioner didn't miss the second time.

A 3-round burst from the FNC did the job neatly as two rounds struck the enemy gunner in the chest and the third ripped away the better part of his jaw. Blood sprayed in all directions as the man's body did an odd pirouette before folding to the cold, unyielding factory floor. Bolan tried to get a sight field on the second target but he could no longer see the Los Negros gunner. To make matters worse, reinforcements were arriving.

One of the gunners must have seen movement because he leveled an AKSU-74 submachine gun and sprayed the immediate area. Bolan considered this new turn of events. The influence of the Sinaloa and Mexican cartels spread far and wide, a fact only a fool would have attempted to disprove. But to see Kalashnikov-grade weapons in the hands of such a group worried the Executioner some. What had he come up against?

Bolan pushed the distraction from his mind, filed it for later reference and then returned fire. He had nothing to lose since his position had somehow become exposed. More rounds from his enemies cut furrows in the cement, sending sharp pieces flying in all directions. A couple even got Bolan in the face and he felt just a trickle of blood begin to run down his cheek. Several more rounds struck the barrels Bolan had used as cover. Most of them were hollow but then Bolan heard one struck by a round, punching a hole through it and producing a very dull sound.

The odor of something dense and acrid, almost noxious, began to assail Bolan's nostrils and then his eyes started to water. At first he thought they'd exposed him to some sort of biohazard agent but Bolan quickly identified the odor as something oddly familiar—paint thinner. That was it. Bolan inspected the barrel and quickly found what he was looking for, a silver stencil on the side of the barrel that read C10H16. Bolan knew it immediately: turpentine. Of course they would need to carry such chemicals on site to destroy any evidence if they were raided by *federales*.

The Executioner grinned at his good fortune as he yanked one of the M-62 grenades from his harness, popped the spoon and let it fly. Bolan burst from cover and the Los Negros crew immediately pursued—just as Bolan hoped—while they paved the way with a steady stream of rounds. Bolan found significant cover behind a thick steel plate that was mounted to a wall and acted as a divider for the monstrous room.

When the M-62 went off, Bolan could feel the heat from the blast as it immediately ignited the turpentine. The fuel had such a high rating of flammability, however, that Bolan knew it would burn extremely hot but wouldn't last for a long time. The best he could hope was that it would spread to the row of processing equipment that, even as he stood there, was humming along and refining Casco's evil and destructive wares. It didn't take any time, and over the crackle of the flames that nearly reached the ceiling Bolan could hear the screams of several of his opponents who had been caught in the direct path of the superheated blast.

Bolan dashed from cover, triggering his weapon on the run as he rushed for a vaulted window on the far side. The Executioner made it to the long table directly below it, scaled it with a single jump and immediately springboarded through the window. The drop outside would have been fairly significant, something Bolan actually expected, except for the fact there happened to be a large aboveground power box immediately beneath the window. Bolan landed on it and then a second jump put him on the ground outside the factory.

Bolan sprinted to the corner of the factory and as he rounded it he spotted the tractor-trailer straight ahead. The warrior reached it in no time flat and immediately dropped the trailer supports—he could make additional distance by leaving the trailer behind. He would have preferred to know the contents but he didn't think it mattered at that point. He'd come to do what he planned, destroying Casco's manufacturing capabilities. With luck, this would hurt Casco's operations and his pocketbook at the same time.

The Executioner had learned early in his war against the Mob that the best strategy against a numerically superior force was to hit those targets that would rob the enemy of both material and fiscal resources. Added to that idea were the psychological effects of swift but spectacular hits against those same resources. This plan ultimately acted upon both the physical and mental pillars of an enemy and crumbled them before its eyes. Bolan had found such tactics to be effective and enduring.

Bolan checked his watch. Nearly ten minutes had passed since he'd parted company with Duke and he was growing concerned. Before he could consider his options, an alarm sounded from within the factory. In a very short time he'd have a group of extremely angry, hostile and well-armed Los Negros hitters on his hands, and he would have preferred to take them with some running room.

As if on cue, Duke and a young, attractive woman suddenly burst from the door through which Bolan had earlier witnessed two men drag a third. They sprinted across the dock and as soon as Duke caught sight of Bolan he smiled.

"You come, you come!" he shouted. "You wait for us!"

"I promised I would," Bolan said. "All aboard!"

Bolan assisted the young boy into the cab, followed by his mother. She had a slim but amply curved figure, and dark curly hair. Bolan could see where her son got his looks. Her eyes were smoky and there were some age lines beginning to appear, a culmination of the dry weather and harsh working conditions she'd probably endured just to keep her family fed.

She gave Bolan a respectable space once they were in the cab, watching him with a bit of trepidation while she held her son and stroked his hair. Mother and child began to babble at each other in Spanish but they were talking so fast and being so animated in their hand movements and facial gestures that Bolan could barely understand a word. He eventually gave up trying and focused on driving them out of there.

As he approached the front gate, Bolan noticed people were starting to exit the building. The alarm he'd heard was probably a fire alarm, perhaps one that had gone off automatically. Bolan's little fire would more than likely consume most, if not all, of the evidence and Casco would probably just file an insurance claim. Well, it didn't matter because for the moment Bolan could take heart in the fact he'd put a significant hurting on Casco.

"You did good, mister!" Duke exclaimed. "You tough."

"We're not out of the woods yet, son," Bolan said.

The words he spoke were almost prophetic as he heard a rattle and then detected the tinkling of rounds against the metal body of the tractor-trailer. Bolan up-shifted and dropped the pedal to the floor. The gates began to fill the view ahead and before the guards knew what was happening Bolan plowed through the gates and tore them from their hinges. The trio of guards in the shack had been so surprised by the move that they didn't have time to react, and Bolan was well out of range for their weapons to be effective.

Bolan poured on all the speed he could muster, confident that they wouldn't be able to pursue him, but also ready for anything that might change.

As usual, it didn't take long for that change to manifest itself. In the rearview mirror, Bolan made out two pairs of headlights and the red taillights of pursuit vehicles reflected by the dust left in the wakes of their courses. Bolan considered the options, wondering if he should try to continue outrunning them. The border was only a mile or two away, and the Executioner figured they could make it before the enemy caught up.

That left just one problem.

Bolan could leave the truck parked on the Mexico side and simply walk across the border into the United States. That would be next to impossible for Duke and his mother, although Bolan figured he could make enough of a case that they could wait with the folks from Homeland Security until Bolan could reach Brognola and arrange for an entry visa under extreme circumstances.

"Those men aren't going to be too forgiving when they catch up with us, Duke. Would you and your mother like to live in the United States?"

"I want to go, I like to go. But I no know about my mom."

"Why don't you ask her?" Bolan prompted gently.

The boy's face brightened as if he hadn't thought of that before, and then he began to jabber at his mother again. The conversation went on for more than a minute, and Bolan was beginning to lose patience. Bolan could understand why the woman would be mistrustful of him, but he couldn't be sure if it was because he was an American or simply that she wasn't sure if he meant her son any harm. At the end of the day, it didn't really matter because Bolan knew just from the raised voices that she had no intention of coming into the U.S.

"She no want to go, mister," Duke finally said. "And if she stay, I stay."

"You could make a better life over there," Bolan said in one last attempt to appeal to the woman. He had no idea if she could understand him or not, but he had to make his best attempt. "You could make a better life for your sons. Both of them."

The woman jabbed her finger at her chest, and then waved at Bolan and said, "This is our home. We are *not* leaving, we stay here."

Bolan nodded and said, "I understand."

As they approached the port of entry, Bolan managed to ditch the truck by making a series of turns in one of the less crowded neighborhoods. He eventually came to a dead end and drove into the shadows of a cluster of trees. He disembarked from the cab and then assisted the woman and Duke, the latter insisting all the way from the cab to the ground that he could do it himself.

Bolan knelt and ruffled Duke's hair. "You take care of yourself, Duke. And your mother."

Without warning, the boy threw his arms around the Executioner's neck and Bolan's heart felt as though it might explode. His life had never afforded him any children of his own. He and April Rose had talked now and again of it, but it always seemed like the time went by so fast, the months turned into years, and with the passage of time they moved further away from the idea.

Bolan finally disentangled the young boy's arms from his neck. "Thanks, amigo."

"Thank you, mister. You a good friend."

Bolan reached into his pocket, grabbed two hundred dollars from the roll and handed the rest to the woman. "Don't go back to that factory. Ever. Get out of this city and go find yourselves a nice, safe place to live. Duke deserves a chance. And so do you."

And without another word, the warrior turned and headed for his own country.

14

Hector Casco looked on the shivering form of the governor of Arizona with tremendous satisfaction.

Salto had delivered her gift-wrapped in ropes, a gag and a blindfold. Casco said nothing to her for a long time when she first arrived at his private hangar on the fringe of the Phoenix airport. In anticipation of her arrival, the cartel boss had left his estate and headed directly to the hangar, ordering the pilot to put in a flight plan for Mexico City. Of course, they weren't going that way, but it didn't matter because Casco had plenty of paid lackeys who would put in all the appropriate paperwork if anyone started poking around.

The fact that he'd been forced into such a rash action didn't bother him as much as not having been able to mitigate some of the damage to his operations. The kidnapping of the Kampp bitch had, of course, become the number-one priority for all law enforcement agencies in the state. The police raids conducted against his core distributors had abated for the moment, and the search for Kampp would buy him time to shut down and relocate what remained. Still, they had done considerable harm to his organization, and it would take a long time to recover.

Casco sat back in the deep, leather seat aboard his jet and

stared at Kampp. He had ordered the removal of her blindfold so that she could see him. She wasn't unattractive with her dark complexion and hair—she appeared to possess some of the finer qualities of Spanish women—though he derived no sensual desires from staring at her. His pleasure was the one of pure victory.

After staring at her a while, her coal-colored eyes burning with hatred for him, Casco rose from his seat and removed a small, sharp knife from his pocket. Her eyes widened a bit and Casco took perverse pleasure in the moment. Finally, he slid the knife between the space just behind her right ear and cut away the gag with a rough jerk. Kampp took a deep, gasping breath and spat bits of lint and dust from her mouth.

"Where are you taking me?" she finally demanded, her voice hoarse from hours of being gagged.

"You'll find out soon enough," Casco said.

He pulled a bottled water from the portable refrigerator and offered some to her but she turned her head away and pursed her lips.

"No?" he said, as if talking to a child who refused to eat their vegetables. "That is too bad. I am trying to be civil, Governor Kampp. May I call you Elizabeth?"

Kampp continued to hold her peace but the fiery stare she offered him made it clear she wouldn't appreciate it.

Casco shrugged with indifference and returned to his seat. He folded his legs, retrieved the tumbler still half-full of iced tequila and looked her in the eyes. "Having dispensed with the pleasantries, I think it's time we discuss the future."

"You don't have a future, you bastard," Kampp said. "When my people find you, and believe me they *will* find you, you're going to spend so many years in prison that your great grand-children will be able to come visit you."

"Silence!" Casco's face reddened to a point that it felt as if his head might explode from the blood rush. He took a moment to regain his cool and then added, "You say another word without my permission, woman, and I'll stuff that gag down your throat, followed by my tool."

Kampp clamped her mouth closed after just a flash of shock registered on her face.

"You had your time to puff and bluster and flaunt your power in front of the television cameras," Casco continued. "And you can see what this has bought you. As I was saying, we need to discuss the future."

Casco had elected not to reveal her life was forfeit, instead deceiving her into believing that he would eventually let her go once they had met his demands. If she knew ahead of time that no matter what happened she wouldn't return to Phoenix alive, she might make a bit of trouble for him and try to escape on her own. If Casco had learned anything about Kampp, it was that she had survival instincts much stronger than many women he'd known. Salto had confirmed this when he told Casco of how she'd fought against his men, and they had to drag her kicking and scratching from her car.

"You meddled where you shouldn't have, bitch. You sent your pigs to interfere with me and now those pricks will have to pay through the nose if they want you back."

"It will never happen," Kampp replied. "My people have strict instructions not to negotiate with criminals or terrorists, and you happen to qualify as both!"

Casco felt an instance of anger and without warning he jumped from his seat and slapped Kampp across the face. Her head recoiled violently from the blow and the echo of his hand against her skin reverberated through the main hold of the jet, even above the noise of the engines. Kampp stared daggers but he didn't let it affect him. He was more angered that he'd sloshed his drink than out of any concern for his captive.

"I told you to keep your mouth shut," Casco said as he took his seat once more. "Maybe a gag won't be effective. Maybe I'll have to cut out your tongue."

Casco could make out her quivering lower lip and the squint

in her eyes as she tried to hold back tears, and it gave him an immense feeling of dominance and satisfaction. This whore had been mouthing off about all the things she planned to do to him when she had her mug plastered across every major network, but she didn't come off so tough when faced with a *superior* adversary. No, she didn't impress Casco in the least.

"Do you know who I am?" he asked, not giving her a chance to reply. "I am the one who haunts all of your worst nightmares. You see I'm a businessman, above all, but I am also a leader of men. Men who must fight a war against those who would attempt to subvert our cause. Like any business, I am concerned only with turning a profit. I do not care how I do that and I have no concern for geographical boundaries.

"There was a man much like me some years ago who attempted something similar but it destroyed him. Do you know why? Because he did not have *vision*. Vision is what separates great leaders from those who get by on mediocrity. Vision is how I have been able to stay one step ahead of your pitiful attempts to subvert my operations. Vision is why men fear me, why they respect me. So you see, it is vision that defines who I am and how I shape my world. I take what I want, and I do so without asking or regrets."

Casco paused to take another slug from his drink and then smacked the empty tumbler onto the table near his seat. "What can I say? Visionary men are often underappreciated for what they do. You cannot possibly know the value of my successes because you don't know what it took me to get here. I *earned* everything that I have. It wasn't given to me. I didn't have the fortune of being born into a family of luxury and privilege."

He tugged at his jacked. "Take this suit, for example. Almost fifteen hundred dollars I paid for these measly bits of cloth. And why, because I needed it? Of course, I could have purchased a much less expensive piece but I chose this one because I spent most of my life wanting such things when they were completely unattainable. There was a time where I didn't know where my next meal would come from. I once stabbed two men considerably larger than me for a few scraps of food thrown out by a local grocer in my home town." Casco waved around him. "Now look, I *own* a private jet."

It was the look in Kampp's eyes that told Casco his words were wasted on the woman. She didn't give a damn about his becoming a self-made success. She didn't care because she *couldn't* care; the woman didn't have the vision he'd talked about. The world was filled with great people of history, Casco's ancestors among them, who had cast the pearls of their wisdom and experience to the uninspired of the world only to see it trampled underfoot like waste.

"What's it matter to you, though?" Casco asked. "I do not think there's much point in sharing any of this with you. You cannot appreciate it. I will restore everything that I have lost this day, and you will eventually be returned to your life unharmed if they pay the ransom. Until that time, you will do as you are told and you will not cause me trouble. I am a decent host but it would not be a good idea to press my tolerance. Remember that you are a prisoner and not a guest."

Casco left off saying more. They would soon be landing at the secret facility he'd named El Castillo, at which point he would lock her away until the time came to dispose of her. He wondered for a time if it wouldn't make more sense to simply kill her immediately and remove any risk she might try to escape or create problems, but he abandoned the idea. He still needed to make a show of listing his "demands." He had to stall the cops long enough to finish withdrawing what remained of his distribution areas, and he expected the only way to buy that time would be to provide them with proof of life. They would demand it, in fact, and if Casco's plan were to succeed he would have to play ball by their terms.

At least for a while.

"CAPTAIN HALL, PLEASE."

"Speaking," Hall said to the voice on the other end of his cell phone.

"Captain, this is Patrolman Nikkels. I was one of the officers ordered into plainclothes to take over the OAR on one Claudia Pacorbo?"

Hall nodded, recalling he'd instructed two men from his unit to perform the "observe and report"—an unofficial term utilized when they decided to put a tail on someone but didn't have a warrant to do so—but they had to let uniforms take over after the kidnapping took place. It was standard procedure to replace units when they had to shift resources, and Hall cursed himself for not pulling the OAR detail sooner. He'd have a hard time justifying the overtime for the two cops.

"Yeah, I don't think that's going to go anywhere, Nikkels. Why don't you guys go ahead and pack it in? Just file your OAR notes with the desk sergeant. I'm going to be wrapped up out here on the new emergency for a while."

"Actually, sir, that's why I'm calling," Nikkels replied. "I think this *may* be going somewhere."

"What do you mean?"

"Well…when we showed up to relieve the detectives, they gave us the case file so we had some basic information on Pacorbo. Seems she's got a pretty good set of beefs on her."

"Yeah, I'm familiar with her background, Nikkels. We're kind of busy here, so cut to the quick if you don't mind."

"Yes, sir…well, we were sitting on this motel room where she checked in when all of a sudden this massive limo pulls up. Out of her room she comes dressed to kill, climbs in and heads straight out of town. We were going to lay off because it almost looked like she might leave the state until the limo took her into the Redsand Estates. You familiar with that area?"

"Yeah, I don't live there but I got some clue. What's the

point? You know, Pacorbo's a high-priced call girl, or at least that's what the social worker who counseled her in the youth offenders program noted on her jacket."

"Well, it looks to us like she's back in the entertainment business because she just got dropped off at this spread that you wouldn't believe."

"The quick, Nikkels, remember? You're drifting."

"Getting there, sir. We ran the address of this place just to see what we came up with. It's listed as the home of record for one Rumaldo Salto."

A silent alarm bell went off in Hall's head. "Salto... Rumaldo Salto. Why do I know that name?"

"You should, sir, most cops who've got your time in, and I don't mean no disrespect sir, but long-term cops should know his name. Salto got sent upstate to do an eight-year stint at the age of nineteen for beating a guy to death in a bar fight. He claimed self-defense, the prosecution yelled murder, and they ended up settling on a manslaughter charge. Eventually, the case got appealed and Salto was kicked at just over sixteen months. It made headlines because the guy he killed was the son of an LAPD cop and attending his freshman year of college here."

"Yeah, sure. I remember, that's why his name rang with me. Salto is nothing but trouble and has been ever since he was a juvie. He did his first strong-arm at fourteen under a gang initiation and cried wolf. We knew he'd be trouble coming up through the department because of his smooth tongue."

But more importantly, it had long been rumored that Salto was a member of the Sinaloa cartel and that he'd gained prominence in the organization for being a courier of information. Couriers were one of the best ideas the cartels had ever come up with. Getting a wiretap was difficult enough, particularly with the judges getting more liberal by the day, but at least it wasn't technically difficult to execute. Hitting a mule and catching him in a compromising conversation with a reporter—the term used by the cartels to identify those who communicated with the top bosses—was extremely difficult to predict. This form of communication made it especially challenging because such meetings took place in secret locations and there were no phones involved. Ever.

"As you may know, sir, Rumaldo Salto is rumored to have ties to—"

"Hector Casco, got it," Hall interrupted. "Nikkels, I want you to listen very carefully to me. You guys sit on that house and make sure nobody leaves. I'll have an army there in no time."

"You think they may have Governor Kampp inside, sir?"

"I don't know, but it's as good a place as any to start. You did good work calling me immediately, Nikkels. If this turns out favorable in any way, I'm going to put both you and your partner in for a commendation if I have to pin the things on your chests myself. Now stand fast and give me twenty minutes."

"Yes, sir. We'll make sure nobody leaves."

IT DIDN'T TAKE HALL any time to get a warrant to enter the premises once he presented his theory to the judge. With the Arizona governor's life on the line, they were willing to sign away just about anything, including their firstborn, if the police had even so much as a hunch as to where the governor might be located. No judge wanted to have to face up to the fact that he or she had refused to sign a warrant for some bureaucratic or technical issue and their actions resulted in a memorial service instead of a homecoming parade for Governor Kampp.

Hall didn't mean to take advantage of that fact in any sense, but he didn't figure he'd have to. He believed, as did most of the men accompanying him, that chances were good Governor Kampp might be inside. And even if she weren't, Hall looked forward to a chance to catch Salto in the act of doing something stupid.

By the time Hall and Murach arrived at the residence in Redsand Estates, the SWAT and DPS Tactical Response Unit were already on scene and in position. Hall would have to surrender the stage to Commander Anthony Stiles of the Arizona DPS-TRU. In a situation involving a state governor, the state police were in charge of all aspects since they were considered, for all intents and purposes, the governor's police. However, the boatload of feds were supposed to arrive soon according to the promise Brognola had made less than an hour earlier.

Stiles was a tall, lanky type with blue eyes and gray-white hair. He had a nose like a hawk's beak and thin lips. He stood over a map spread on a field table and for a minute, Hall couldn't help but wonder what the hell he'd need with a map of the surrounding area. It was an upper-class neighborhood, for chrissake. How the hell was that going to help him? Oh, well, live and let live, Hall thought. It wasn't until he got closer he realized the map was of the residence itself and not the development.

"What's the story?" Hall asked Stiles as soon as he arrived.

"I've got a sniper unit in three separate positions across the street. They tell me they have a clean field of fire across most of the property. As to the house itself, it's decorated in the traditional style of southwest Spanish, so there are vigas, porticos and a bunch of other similar architecture."

"We know who owns this place?"

Stiles shrugged. "Apparently, the place was bought and paid for by Principal Industry Investments, Inc. as a bonus for the company's CEO, Roberto Gonzales."

"Roberto Gonzales?" Hall thought the name sounded familiar, but couldn't place it. "Have we made contact with anyone inside yet?"

"Not so far, but I'm about to order a reconnoiter of surrounding houses, talk to other residents and see if we can collect any additional info."

"I wouldn't waste the time if I were you," Hall said. "If Governor Kampp is inside the house, I say we move in hard and fast without fucking around. This thing could go straight to dog shit if we wait too long."

"It might, then it might not, Captain. But with all due respect, sir, I'm in charge here and I don't plan to just send our men in there without having as good an idea as I can of what I'm up against."

Hall cocked his head and raised his hands in a gesture of surrender. "Okay, you're right, this is your show. I'm going to back off. I just figured maybe you'd like to hear my take on this out of the spirit of cooperation."

"Understood, Captain. And like I say, no offense and I truly mean it." Stiles wiped at his neck, groaning with the obvious stiffness in it. "Damn it all, but I wish we had more information."

Hall didn't know how to respond to that. If he'd been allowed to become involved in the operation he would have been satisfied, but the only thing he'd managed to do was get a warrant. They were leaving the hard-core tactical response to the big guns, and it bothered Hall on one level because he felt a bit responsible for some of what had transpired to this point. In either case, Stiles would make his move at the time he dictated and Hall could only hope it happened really soon.

The clock was ticking down.

15

John Udolf Grimaldi, aka Jack, had just finished performing his postflight inspection when he saw the approach of a familiar form.

Grimaldi grinned at the long figure when he was still some distance from the plane. The pilot stuck his hand out as they met, the man shaking his hand with a firm and steady grip. The two stood and watched each other for a moment, and then Bolan nodded his acknowledgment. Grimaldi understood the gesture. Bolan was glad to see him, no doubt about it, but he'd learned his friend was a man of few words and rarely spoke of his feelings. Not that Bolan didn't feel—of course he felt, like all living beings. Some had thought Bolan brooding, even introverted, but that just proved their ignorance.

Bolan was one of the most...*sensitive* men Grimaldi had ever had the pleasure of knowing.

Since their alliance first forged on the rooftop of a Las Vegas casino, Grimaldi had acquired a level of respect and admiration he had for few others. In fact, Grimaldi had really come to view the men and women of Stony Man as family and Bolan as sort of the mature eldest brother in the bunch, the one who took the rest of his siblings under his wing. The commanding presence of the Executioner made others around him feel better, more confident in themselves, but it also demanded unflinching respect. And Bolan had never asked Grimaldi for more than his esteem and friendship, both of which the pilot had submitted willingly.

Grimaldi had been working for the Mafia with no sense of pride or respect for himself, and then along came the Executioner to change his mind. Of course, Grimaldi had first seen Bolan as an enemy but that quickly dissolved. Grimaldi had known all along that the life he'd chosen to live wasn't the right one, wasn't the one for which he'd been destined. It had been Bolan who'd shown him his error and given Grimaldi the courage to leave the Mob, do something better for himself and his country.

Grimaldi looked back on that time with absolutely no regrets.

"Damned good to see you, Sarge," he said around his cigar.

"Ditto," Bolan replied. "Thanks for coming, Ace. Really."

"You look wiped out, big guy."

"I feel it."

Grimaldi clapped him on the back as they started for the plane. "Well, I sure to hell wish I could offer better news, but there have been some developments."

Bolan frowned. "This doesn't sound good."

"It's not. Sarge, Governor Elizabeth Kampp has been kidnapped."

"When?"

"A few hours ago. The Farm tried to contact you but I guess your mobile receiver's not working. Even I couldn't reach you."

Bolan nodded and withdrew his phone from the pouch on his belt—or what was left of it. The unit had been clipped by a bullet during Bolan's battle with the Los Negros fighters at the factory, and he hadn't realized it until changing civvies. If he'd had the luxury of time, he could have waited for some sort of diplomatic credentials to get him across the border, since crossing in a blacksuit with an assortment of weapons and ordnance dangling from his LBE wouldn't have gone over very well with customs officials. But the clock was ticking—faster and louder. Bolan had been forced to stow the equipment in his butt pack, get a cab to take him back to his rental, and then change into civvies and bury the weaponry in the desert before crossing over into American territory.

Grimaldi took the phone, inspected it and then shook his head with a grin. "Ouch, don't think that's covered under the warranty."

"Right," Bolan said. "Do we have a possible location on Kampp?"

"Only a theory, but it sounds pretty solid."

Once they were aboard the plane, Grimaldi pulled up the information transmitted by Stony Man Farm to their onboard computers. He bent over near the Executioner, who was seated in front of the LCD monitor that displayed a terrain map of Nogales. Grimaldi gestured toward an area marked with a red circle. "There's a small mountain range about sixteen klicks northwest of Nogales. This Hector Casco character has some kind of hidey-hole he's built himself here, at this point. Apparently, an undercover DEA agent reported it a number of years ago but it got filed away by a clerk and nobody ever paid much attention to it. Barb and Hal think that's Casco's most likely destination."

"We have anything more to lead us to this point?"

Grimaldi stood and scratched his neck. "Not really. Barb said you might ask, too, and she wanted me to tell you that Casco had originally built the place as a retreat in case the head of the Sinaloa cartel discovered what he was up to. They've been monitoring flights out of Phoenix and surrounding airports. So far, we don't have anything. There was one private flight, some corporation, that left Phoenix a couple of hours ago but its flight plan was for Mexico City and according to computer records it arrived as scheduled."

Bolan shook his head. "Means nothing. Casco has the clout and money to have someone make false entries in the logs. That flight's exactly what I was looking for. Barb and Hal did good work on this one."

"So you think that Casco actually went to Mexico City with Governor Kampp?"

"No, I think he's gone exactly where the Farm says he has. He just wants everyone to *think* he's gone to Mexico City."

"Ah."

"I also think we're running on borrowed time here, Ace. How long before you can be underway."

"Few minutes," Grimaldi said. As he turned and headed for the cockpit he added, "I've already done a preflight so we're ready to go. Just let me get clearance on the horn and we'll be airborne in no time."

"Thanks," Bolan called. "I'll contact the Farm."

Bolan quickly committed the terrain surrounding Casco's stronghold to memory, confident he'd have to make a HALO jump on this go-around. Not that it would pose a problem for Grimaldi or the plane. This new Gulfstream C-38A, the military designation for the civilian version known as a G100, had recently been outfitted to meet Stony Man's stringent requirements. It boasted a complete armory and medical supply unit concealed within a fold-up panel, as well as a full array of electronic and countersurveillance equipment built between the interior walls and the fuselage that utilized fiber-optic technology. The newly acquired jet sported a pair of Honeywell TFE 731 engines that could take it a range of nearly 3,000 nautical miles at a ceiling of 45,000 feet.

Of course, Bolan wouldn't have to make his HALO jump from that height. Developed by the U.S. Air Force in the 1960s, a high-altitude, low-open jump was a military free-fall technique where the parachutist deployed from 25,000 to

35,000 feet but did not open the chute until very low, maybe 2,000 at most. HALO jumps differed considerably from a standard military deployment as performed by airborne troops throughout the world. In that instance the chute opened almost as soon as the paratrooper left the plane, the jump was usually at about 1,500 feet and the jumper typically reached the ground in under a minute.

Bolan keyed up the computer, engaged the webcam and within a minute he was looking into the lovely, blue eyes of Barbara Price.

"Hey, stranger," she said. "Are you okay? We—"

"Sorry, but I'll have to save the explanations for later. I'm with Eagle and he's brought me up to speed. I think you guys are right on the money about Casco."

"Good, I was hoping your assessment would agree with ours."

"Have there been any demands?"

"No, not yet," Price said. She frowned and added, "Frankly, I'm concerned there won't be. If Hector Casco did kidnap her, our chances of finding her alive and in good condition are minimal. He might just kill her for the fun of it."

Bolan shook his head. "I don't think so. I think Casco has plans to use her in the same way he's used so many other people."

"What do you mean?"

"Casco's not running scared, here. If he did kidnap the governor, and I believe he did because that's just his style, he has some backup plan put into place. My guess is he's stalling for time, although I can't be certain yet what his reasons are."

"Maybe it's a diversion, an attempt to take the heat off his operations in Phoenix," Price offered.

"That's possible, I hadn't considered it before. It might be something more, like maybe he's trying to impress the heads of his cartel, over perhaps even attempting to seize control.

Governor Kampp would certainly be a worthy prize to wield under the right circumstances."

"Well, whatever the case is, I don't suppose it will change your approach."

"No," Bolan said. "I'll do a high-altitude insertion into his camp, locate the governor and get out of there quick. I also plan to destroy Casco's little hideaway if time permits. And if I can get close enough, Casco along with it."

"Hold on a second, Striker," Price interjected. "Bear's telling me we have some new intelligence coming in from Phoenix. Hold up and I'll put him on."

The screen went blank a moment and then Price's face was replaced by the bearded visage of Aaron Kurtzman. "What do you say, big guy?"

"Hey, Bear. Talk to me."

"Okay, we just got word that this Captain Hall accompanied a team of local and state tactical units onto the grounds of Casco's Redsand Estates residence. They were apparently following some prostitute named Claudia Pacorbo. Ring any bells?"

Bolan shook his head at first and then something jogged his memory. "Wait a minute, Hall *did* mention her. Something about she'd been beaten up, and then given money and told to leave the state."

"Well, I don't know anything about that but apparently they ran the address she went to and got a hit on Rumaldo Salto, a known player in the Sinaloa cartel and associate of Hector Casco."

"What went down?"

"There was a pretty intense gun battle and several casualties on the side of the cops, although no fatalities," Kurtzman said.

"Good to hear."

"And another tidbit of interesting news, maybe the crème de la crème of it all. Remember how you were telling me about Casco, how he was mostly a ghost and all we had was a fifteen-year-old photo?"

"Yeah?"

"Well that's because Casco's been using a cover identity here in the United States for more than a decade. Seems a big-time entrepreneur among the wealthiest socialites in America. He's been going by the name Roberto Gonzales. He owns a half-dozen companies. Pays his taxes, has a driver's license and even supposedly is married with two children. Of course, they're never seen because he has them in private schools overseas, or so that's how he explains it, and his wife is very reclusive and does not wish to be seen in public."

"What about Salto?" Bolan asked. "What's his status?"

"Unfortunately or fortunately, depending on how you look at it, Salto is deceased. Sitting in a cooler down at the Phoenix city morgue by now, I'd imagine. He shot it out with the cops when they hit Casco's residence. He lost. Word has it that it was Joe Hall who got him."

"Any sign of Casco?"

"No, but apparently Pacorbo gave it all up and confirmed she had affiliations with Casco. She's agreed to turn state's evidence in trade for immunity from prosecution once Casco's apprehended."

"Tell Hal he ought to contact the prosecutor and suggest he rethink making any deals," Bolan said. "Pacorbo had her chance and Casco isn't going to live to be apprehended anyway. Not if I have anything to say about it."

"And you definitely do, my friend."

"Okay, I'll be in touch as soon as I've retrieved Governor Kampp."

"Understood. And Barb also wanted me to pass on the Man's personal thanks for getting involved with this one. He's authorized whatever it takes to bring the governor home alive."

Bolan nodded. "Let him know I'll do my best. Out, here."

The Executioner disconnected the transmission and immediately headed to the hidden armory. He exposed the concealed keypad in the ceiling compartment, punched in his fifteen-digit access code and the wall slid aside to reveal enough weapons and ordnance to start a small war. In fact, that was exactly what Bolan had planned. The first step would be to get inside the perimeter undetected. He'd be making the jump in the dark so split-second timing would be crucial at the actual moment of deployment. Not that it would be a problem. With Grimaldi at the stick, Bolan would know exactly when to leap and he could take the rest of it from there.

A HALO jump had the distinct advantage of preventing an enemy from pinpointing the target because the parachutist traveled at incredible speed. Infrared sensors could detect jumpers simply by the friction building around from the fall, but that required extremely sensitive equipment and Bolan doubted Casco had anything quite so sophisticated in his arsenal. There wouldn't be a lot of time once he reached ground zero. He'd have to get in and out as quickly as possible. Retrieving Elizabeth Kampp alive was the priority, and Bolan had to remind himself that he might have to save Casco for another day.

Bolan quickly stripped out of his civvies and climbed into the insulated, aerodynamic HALO suit, a special rip-stop nylon blend coupled with a polypropylene liner to prevent frostbite. He then donned the special positive-pressure apparatus and helmet that would protect him from the wicked thin air and prevent lung collapse. Once he had his equipment in place, Bolan engaged the prebreather tank attached to his suit and donned a mask that would deliver 100 percent oxygen to his bloodstream. He would have to breathe this for at least thirty minutes prior to the jump in order to flush the nitrogen from his system and mitigate the risks of caisson disease from the rapid descent.

As he breathed the oxygen, Bolan began a weapons check.

He decided to leave the Beretta 93-R behind in favor of the Desert Eagle .44 Magnum. He expected to need some decent firepower and he had weight considerations given he was making a HALO jump this go-around. Had he been deploying from low-altitude he probably wouldn't have thought anything of it. Additionally, the Executioner selected a pair of MP-5 K machine pistols over an assault rifle; again, a weight and profile consideration took precedence.

Bolan selected a quartet of Diehl DM-51 hand grenades with some glee. He'd come to appreciate the versatile uses provided by this ordnance. The Stony Man teams had also put the grenades to significantly good use. Designed and manufactured by an Austrian firm, the DM-51 featured a plastic cylinder at the center loaded with HE filler. A wraparound sleeve filled with steel balls could be attached readily or removed from the body core at will, which gave the DM-51 either offensive or defensive capabilities, as the conditions dictated. Additionally, the grenades could be attached to one another to form a significant charge.

The Executioner completed the arsenal with a satchel containing forty quarter-pound sticks of C-4 plastique explosive and a handful of detonators. This would provide Bolan with enough ordnance to create significant destruction and chaos while he made off with their captive. The time moved so quickly in Bolan's preparations that before he knew it he was being signaled by Grimaldi from the cockpit.

"Go, Ace," Bolan said.

"I'm circling the target now for a pass. Looks like we're a go, Sarge. You ready?"

"Roger that. Lower the ramp and I'll take position."

The "ramp" was a small rear hatch in the aft portion of the plane from which Bolan could make the HALO. The position of the standard cabin door wasn't practical to jumping, particularly since the C-38 hadn't been designed for tactical operations of this nature and a loss in cabin pressure did relatively crazy things to the craft's dynamics at that altitude. This had necessitated a modification in the design to suit Stony Man's purposes. This way, Bolan could make a free-fall jump without worrying about striking the aircraft itself, and without requiring a complete depressurization of the cabin.

"In position," Bolan said when he'd sealed the cabin hatch over him and lowered the ramp.

"Roger that," Grimaldi's voice came back. "You reading me?"

"Five by five, Ace."

"Okay, in five seconds…four…three…ready…*go!*"

Bolan let himself fall through the hatch, body tucked so that he and his equipment cleared it. Despite the special suit he could feel the intense cold biting at him, and he watched the condensation form on his face shield. It would clear in a moment, he knew, so Bolan didn't panic when his visibility dropped to nothing. True to form, the shield cleared after about ten seconds and Bolan checked the altimeter attached to his wrist. The hands in the red glow provided information on Bolan's distance from the ground, average vertical drop velocity and a signal preprogrammed to go off when he reached three thousand feet.

Bolan enjoyed the view, relished the rush of air that whispered in his ears even with the protective helmet in place. HALO jumps were the quietest moments he could ever remember in his life. No gunfire, nobody in need and generally a period of communications blackout per SOP. HALO jumps required all of the parachutist's attention and that dictated nobody yakking in the jumper's ear while he focused on getting to the ground in one piece.

The moment was short-lived, however, and within two minutes Bolan saw the light go from yellow to green. Bolan pulled the rip cord and braced for the sudden jolt that would yank him upward before he began re-descent. While it played havoc a bit on the shoulders, Bolan always looked forward to that jerking sensation because it signaled successful chute deployment. When it came, Bolan made sure his lips were closed, tongue pressed tightly against the roof of his mouth so he didn't bite it.

The last thousand feet gave Bolan a fairly decent view and he smiled when noticing he'd come down within two hundred yards of Casco's hidden stronghold. Not that it was really hidden that well. Bolan could see the twinkle of lights; there were only a few but they were present and visible even through the canopy of trees. Which brought Bolan to his next consideration, although not one he hadn't given thought to. Bolan had known his chances of landing in an open space were slim, but this time Fate smiled on him.

The Executioner dropped into a clearing about eighty yards in total diameter. He touched down gracefully, bending his knees and preparing for the impact. As soon as he felt his feet hit the ground, Bolan tucked and rolled along his thigh, hip and shoulder. His body came down in a picture-perfect landing for a paratrooper, just as Bolan had been trained to do, and done in real operations many times before.

Unfortunately, nature had something to say about it, too. Bolan grunted as his right side hit what must have been a rock jutting from the ground. The impact sent sharp, shooting pains into his side and Bolan knew in a moment, even as he completed his roll and came to his feet, that he'd fractured at least two ribs. Bolan snapped the quick release clamps for the chute, then took a knee and clenched his teeth to fight the pain that jabbed every time he inhaled.

The Executioner let a few minutes lapse before finally reaching into his pack and withdrawing a field compress. He placed the bulky side against his rib, wrapped it tightly around his chest to stabilize the area and then flipped the switch that would engage the radio system of the suit coded on a special frequency linked directly with the communications system aboard the C-38.

"Striker to Eagle One."

"Eagle One, here, Striker," Grimaldi's voice came back immediately.

"I'm down but some bumps."

"You still in the game?" Grimaldi asked, concern evident in his tone.

"Roger that. Proceed to Lima Zulu Gamma as planned. I'll meet you there in nine-zero minutes."

They had agreed that Bolan would bring Kampp out and Grimaldi would touch down in a makeshift airstrip utilized by DEA and narcotics officers of the Mexican government approximately two klicks south of Casco's jungle stronghold. The strip had been seized by the Mexican government a few years earlier after they managed to bring down a major ring. It seemed almost poetic justice that they chose to maintain the thing. It would take a while for anybody to know Grimaldi was using it, and with luck they would be long gone before Mexican officials arrived to investigate.

Bolan steeled his mind against the nagging, stabbing sensation in his ribs as he concealed his jump gear, stripped out of his suit and set off toward the hardsite.

The game clock had started running, sure.

But the Executioner was ready.

16

Elizabeth Kampp ultimately didn't get to see where they had taken her.

Before the plane landed, her captor had put a new blindfold on her and two men roughly escorted her from the plane to a vehicle. They had driven about an hour or so, she was guessing, to some location. Once they arrived, she was stripped to only her panties. The men who took her clothes had whispered and laughed with one another in Spanish. They didn't know she spoke it fluently, but she tried not to react as they openly discussed violating her.

Fortunately, the man that had been so cruel to her aboard the plane intervened and warned them sternly not to consider such a thing.

Kampp was relieved although it wasn't as if she felt any real gratitude toward the man. He was simply keeping her in decent shape purely as an insurance policy. Her people would never negotiate for her release if they had any inkling she was dead or severely maimed. This banal and self-involved maniac who had kidnapped her was obviously intelligent enough to know it wouldn't buy him any consideration whatsoever from the American government if he allowed his men to abuse her in any way.

Which brought her to another question: exactly who was this son of a bitch? Outside of being a short, ugly, foul-mouthed Hispanic male with a Napoleon complex, Kampp couldn't come up with a name to fit the face. She figured he was part of one of the Mexican drug cartels since she had just been to a press conference and spoken of the imminent crackdown on the kidnappers and drug dealers running rampant through the city.

Warned by the man to leave her be, the men traded Kampp's clothing for attire that felt abrasive against her skin. She wanted to scratch everywhere and it drove her batty since they left her blindfolded and hands bound. She ultimately ended up in some sort of cell, although she did believe it was outdoors. She could hear the sounds of animals in the surrounding jungle, and when first brought here she'd been led into a structure that was powered and air-conditioned.

Eventually, she'd been "prepped" and dumped in this muggy, swampy hellhole. Kampp listened for the sound of human company but to no avail. Only the call of birds and insects—joined by a cacophony of eerie sounds she'd never heard before—reached her ears. Sweat trickled down every crevice of her body, causing her to experience a variety of sensations when she let her imagination begin to run away with her and fear set in.

Kampp eventually talked herself down, trying to quiet her mind, but she'd catch herself falling asleep and that would eventually cause her to return to a lucid state. She didn't want to sleep away the last few hours of her life, if it was going to come to that.

The governor tried to keep her focus on her present predicament. When she first entered law school, she had taken a course in kidnapping cases as one of her electives. She had originally planned to practice law for a few years before running for public office, and she knew she'd be serving mostly wealthy politicians and families with varied levels of public notoriety. Because of that fact, she would need to have experience negotiating with kidnappers since wealthy families were often targets of that particular criminal enterprise, and just as often they turned to their lawyers to negotiate terms of ransom or other demands rather than go to the FBI.

Kampp had always figured the number of kidnappings in Phoenix and the greater metro area were much higher than statistics suggested. Those kidnappings could only be known if they were recorded. Kampp had to wonder what the *real* number was, and how many families had paid off ransom demands or satisfied other requests rather than involving law enforcement. She couldn't very well blame them. Most families, even wealthy ones, didn't have the ability to call on the kinds of resources that were probably mobilizing at that very moment in response to her own kidnapping.

Kampp knew that if the demands were made directly of her husband, Henry, he would do whatever he had to in securing her release.

And then Kampp stifled the sudden urge to cry, to let off all the stress that she'd been pushing deep inside of her. She hoped no one could hear her—she didn't want them to think she was afraid of them. But Kampp wept for the thought she might not see Henry or her children again. She also wept for the deaths of Beau and Marcus. And she wept for all the citizens who had believed in her when just earlier that day she'd told them they had no reason to fear.

What utter rot!

Well, it no longer mattered because she doubted very much her captor would let her go. Eventually Kampp's crying died off and rage replaced it. She hated the murderous bastard who had taken the lives of two of her best staff. She felt a tinge of concern for her family, as well, uncertain if he'd arranged to kidnap any of them. That would give him an even better negotiating position if he had multiple members of the Kampp family to work with. Kampp dismissed the idea, convinced she had been his first and only play.

Kampp began to think through her options. She could fake an illness, wait until they came to investigate and then try to overpower them. She dismissed the thought just as quickly, telling herself, *This isn't television, Liz. You're not James Bond or something.* Kampp began to explore other options, each one wilder than the first, but eventually she realized the futility of it all. No, she wasn't going anywhere.

Then she heard something, something that sounded like movement. Kampp held her breath, her heartbeat quickening and the pulse thudding in her ears. She got angry with herself, forcing her breathing to a slower pace to try to decrease her racing heart so she could hear. What was that? A scratching sound? Maybe there was a wild animal near her outdoor prison. Was she exposed? Had they put her outside in the hopes some sort of lion or something would come along and snack on her body? Maybe they had scented her clothes with something to attract the beasts of the jungle.

Oh, get a *hold* of yourself, Liz. You're letting your imagination get away with you.

No, but there was a noise and she couldn't quite place it. And then she started to hear it again, this time moving a little faster, almost at a frenetic pace, but with detectable regularity. Yet she could not be sure she heard anything, and if she *was* hearing this noise legitimately, she could not be certain what it meant.

So Kampp did the only thing she could.

She listened. And waited.

Then suddenly, before she could react, a hand clamped over her mouth and she heard a voice whisper in her ear. "Governor Kampp, don't cry out, I'm here to help you."

BOLAN FLEXED THE MUSCLES in his forearm as he sawed at the thick ropes that Casco's men had used to build the hot box.

When Bolan had reached the perimeter, he performed a full sweep and that's when he discovered the makeshift prison. Bolan had seen many such structures before and he knew exactly what it was. The hot box produced not only a psychological effect on prisoners, exposing them to hot weather, mosquitoes and other jungle elements, but it also provided a measure of additional security. Anyone attempting a rescue would naturally search the main house first, and that would provide Casco and his men an opportunity to come here and terminate their prize before anyone got to her.

What they hadn't banked on was that the Executioner wasn't just anyone. He'd played this game plenty of times before, enough that he'd acquired almost a sixth sense about his enemies. Bolan knew just about every trick in the book—he wouldn't have been effective for this long, otherwise—so it didn't take more than a moment to realize that Governor Kampp was right where most wouldn't have ever expected.

Bolan didn't speak to her even once he realized she was inside. He wanted a crack at Casco and he'd never get it if he revealed himself to Kampp before the time was right. Instead, Bolan went right to work on the heavy ropes used to bind the thick four-by-four-inch square poles to each other. The teeth on the back side of Bolan's KA-BAR fighting knife were a bit thick for the job but he didn't want to dull the blade against the wood, so he sawed with regular even pressure until the ropes frayed and eventually came apart.

The work proved time-consuming at best, but Bolan had enough rope cut away to provide a decent-sized egress in just under five minutes. Bolan then stripped off his harness and slid through the opening. Kampp sat on the far side of the hut with her back to the wall. Bolan moved over to her and gently placed a hand on her mouth.

"Governor Kampp, don't cry out," he whispered in her ear. "I'm here to help you."

She nodded slowly and Bolan backed his hand off.

"Who are you?"

"Consider me the cavalry."

"You…you're trying to trick me."

"I'm not," Bolan said. "How can I prove it to you?"

"Well, if you're who I *think* you are, what's the name of the guy at the Justice Department who called me this morning?"

"His name's Brognola."

"You know him then?"

"Almost as well as I know myself. Are you satisfied?"

He could see her smile in the darkness. "You bet I am. And if we get out of here alive I want to talk to you about shooting up the city of Phoenix."

"Couldn't be helped," Bolan mumbled. "Listen very carefully. I'm not going to take you out of here yet."

"What?"

"You have to understand that I have a little business with the man who took you. There's the matter of a score that *must* be settled. He owes for all the murdering, dope peddling and kidnapping he's been doing and I plan to end that here and now."

"Your first duty is to get me out of here," Kampp insisted.

"No disrespect intended, Governor, but you don't decide that. I do." On afterthought he added, "And keep your voice down or neither one of us will leave here except feet first."

"So you're going to just leave me here to fend for myself."

Bolan shook his head and then cut her bonds and removed the blindfold. She blinked hard a few times, trying to clear the stars from the pressure caused by the blindfold being a little tight. She then focused on him and Bolan let her get a good look before he spoke.

"I've freed you. You can run, if you want, but I doubt you'll get very far through the jungle at night." Bolan considered what he could do to ease her anxiety while she waited. Finally, he said, "You ever fire a gun before, Governor Kampp?"

"My father used to take me to the pistol range sometimes."

Bolan nodded and detached one of the MP-5 Ks. He jacked the slide to the rear, validated the hammer home on a round and then pressed it into her hand. "This is an MP-5 K, a 9 mm machine pistol. It has thirty rounds in the magazine. If you aim at someone, you squeeze the trigger and that will cause a short burst. Never hold it down or you'll burn up your ammunition very quickly."

"And then what?"

Bolan frowned. "If anyone's left standing, you're dead."

Kampp's complexion paled some, visible even in the dark. "Oh...I see."

"Stay put and don't make a sound. I'll be back to get you in a few minutes and then we'll go home. You understand?"

"But I don't want to stay here by myself. I'm afraid."

Bolan tried to smile. "I understand, Governor, believe me."

"You know, I'd prefer if you just call me Elizabeth. I'm not really feeling very governor-like at the moment anyway. And since it would appear I owe you my life, we can probably skip the formalities."

"I'll keep it in mind. But the fact remains that things in Phoenix are never going to get better as long as this guy's around."

"Who is he anyway?"

"I'll explain later," Bolan said. "I have to go."

The Executioner rose, turned and quickly exited through the opening he'd made. He donned his harness and then skirted the perimeter of trees until he could get as close to the main house as possible without exposing his position. That still put him nearly fifty yards from the structure, a pretty good distance to cross even in the dark. He'd be vulnerable to just about anything and everything the enemy could throw at him. Then again, he'd be vulnerable no matter what the distance.

Bolan checked the remainder of the grounds as far as he could see and his flank before bursting from cover and sprinting across the open space. He reached the fringes of the house unmolested and pressed his back to the exterior wall. The adobe-style wall felt warm against his back, still holding the heat of the day. Sweat slicked his forehead and his fatigues had begun to cloyingly stick to his body from the sweat and humidity.

The Executioner started to formulate his plan for placing the ordnance when something caught his attention. Something he had heard many times before, something that caused every hair on his neck to come to attention. A cold lump of something like fear hit his stomach and seemed to spread over every inch of his body, reaching even to his fingers and toes like a surge of electricity.

Yeah, he knew that sound.

The growl of a trained guard dog.

17

Bolan froze and anticipated his next move.

The growl seemed low and sustained, coming from just over his shoulder. The Executioner slowly turned his head and peered in that direction. Sure enough, he spotted the dog—a large Doberman pinscher with lighter brown patches around his feet and muzzle—with its cropped ears held back and muscular body standing slightly forward in a classic pose of alertness. The dog's eyes locked on Bolan's and he emitted another growl.

Bolan's hand reached ever so slowly toward the Desert Eagle in military webbing on his hip. He managed to disengage the safety strap and wrap his hand around the thick butt of the pistol before the dog went into motion. There wasn't much room for error and Bolan got the weapon cleared just in time to expose the butt.

And then the dog was on him, immediately going for his throat. Bolan knew the poor animal was only doing as it was trained, and given those circumstances he almost never took lethal action against a creature unless left with no choice. Fortunately, he didn't feel this was one of those times. Bolan stuck his forearm into the air and this distracted the Doberman enough to get his fangs around the meatiest portion. The sharp canines immediately sunk into his flesh and drew blood, but it also provided the distraction needed. Better a couple of small holes in his forearm than his throat ripped to shreds.

The soldier turned and knelt, whipping the dog around with him as he moved and slamming its body against the earth. This forced the dog to exhale and that natural reaction caused its jaws to slacken. Bolan then followed with a pistol butt to the flank of the animal's skull. He repeated twice more before it completely rendered the Doberman unconscious. The blows had been to specific cranial nerves that helped control its balance and equilibrium.

Bolan got to his feet, winded and bleeding but thankful to be alive, and inspected his arm. The sleeve of his jungle cammies was torn but not significantly. It was completely soaked with blood, however, and Bolan became concerned the dog might have gotten a small artery. He reached into his med-pouch, removed his second and final field dressing and quickly bound his forearm. The warrior then moved back to his original position and took a moment to rest. Through some miracle, nobody had heard the commotion on the lawn. They were probably inside, laughing and drinking it up, and congratulating Casco and each other for their perceived victory.

Well, the Executioner didn't mind providing some of the fireworks for their celebration. Bolan quickly searched the side and back of the house until he came upon the external junction panel. He removed the flimsy lock-clip with the assistance of the KA-BAR, and planted his first two sticks of C-4 to the base of the box, attached the radio-controlled fuse and then closed the panel.

Bolan continued his search until he found a rear entrance. It surprised him that Casco would have built such a facility and then not equipped it with sentries. Then again, the cartel underboss probably assumed he was safe here in the middle of nowhere. He likely figured nobody knew about this place other than a select few, not to mention that Phoenix law enforcement wouldn't even know it was him responsible for the attack. As far as Casco was concerned, his identity as Roberto Gonzales, wealthy socialite and generous donator to worthwhile causes, remained intact.

But he couldn't hide from Bolan. And the Executioner was about to blow that identity wide open.

RICKY PRECIADO CRACKED his fourth Tecate and chucked the bottle cap on the table.

"Take it easy on those, *vato*," Rico Cazuela said. "You know what Hector said. Don't be getting all fucked up. We need to keep our heads on straight, keep our eyes on the Kampp bitch until Hector can get this thing squared away."

Preciado took a deep pull from the longneck bottle and then set it loudly on the table as he smacked his lips. "Relax, will you, Rico? You're too wound up, man. I can handle myself. Besides, the boss is in bed and there ain't nobody out here. We're by ourselves, remember?"

"I remember," Cazuela said, dealing them a new hand as a pot of about two hundred dollars sat in the center of the table awaiting the victor. "I'll just be glad when we can off that bitch and get back to more civilized surroundings. This living out in the middle of nowhere drives me crazy. I need to be around people, man, you know? I'm a people person."

This brought a laugh from Preciado. "Since when?"

Cazuela didn't reply, instead he gave his partner a dirty look before fanning his cards and deciding what kind of a chance to take. Neither of the men heard the sliding glass door in the next room open, nor did they know that in the next few moments they would encounter what some considered to be the most dangerous creature on the planet.

BOLAN CAME THROUGH the patio door, surprised to find it unlocked. Sloppiness could be a soldier's best friend, and in this case it was. The Executioner moved inside and put his back to the wall, Desert Eagle up and tracking the area ahead. He stopped to listen and heard voices in the adjoining room, which from the entryway Bolan could see was a kitchen. Bolan waited a minute longer, ensuring the kitchen occupants hadn't heard him enter, and then he went to work setting up a couple of charges against one of the corner supports.

The ordnance placed, Bolan advanced through the room and found a door leading out of the living area and away from the kitchen. It opened onto a hallway. Bolan proceeded down the hall that opened onto a broad, open-ceiling area that served as a foyer. The lights were out here save for a small lamp on a table near the massive front door. Bolan checked his flank and then found a staircase and ascended it quietly. To his surprise, the steps didn't squeak.

Bolan reached the second landing that consisted of a rail and banister overlooking the foyer and a hall beyond that decorated in conventional Spanish style. Latino artwork hung from the walls, and it looked as though the place was painted in reds, browns and other rich earth tones.

The Executioner heard the movement behind him a moment too late to react. A forearm snaked around his neck and yanked back hard, immediately cutting off his windpipe and life-giving oxygen. Bolan cursed himself for allowing the enemy to take him off guard like that. But he could save the self-recrimination for later. At the moment, he needed to deal with this problem before he blacked out. The pressure was significant although it didn't seem Bolan's opponent was that large. Bolan whipped his head to one side to take the pressure off his windpipe, and then drove the heel of his boot into his opponent's shin. Simultaneously, he wedged the flat of his hand between the attacker's bicep and neck.

The move caused his opponent to release him and the Executioner stepped around, bringing an uppercut from the knees. The rock-hard punch connected with enough force to lift his considerably smaller opponent off the ground and send him crashing into a curio cabinet against one wall. The noise would certainly alert the occupants on the first floor that Bolan had managed to avoid. Bolan had maybe a minute to deal with his attacker before the whole house guard, however many that might be, engaged him.

His opponent sprang to his feet and a knife seemed to appear out of nowhere. Bolan took a preparatory stance as the man jumped forward. In the dim light from below he caught just a glimpse of the man's face, and at that point he was certain he was facing off with none other than Hector Casco. Bolan decided to play his hand.

"End of the line, Casco."

"So you know who I am," Casco replied. "I know who you are, too."

Casco jumped forward and tried to stab Bolan in the gut but it was only a feint to keep the Executioner off edge. Bolan didn't fall for it, instead stepping back and sideways to bring his foot into position.

"You're fast, *Diablo en Negro.* But you are not invincible. I know of your exploits against Jose Carillo but I will not fall like he did. Because I am a man of vision."

"No," Bolan replied. "You're a victimizer, Casco. A predator who needs to be excised from the fabric of society. And I'm here to do the surgery."

Casco's face flushed, visible even around his dark complexion, and he charged with fury and tried to slash Bolan's neck. The warrior had waited for the advantage and he finally had it, stepping off line as he connected his boot to the side of Casco's leg at the knee joint. A loud pop resounded in the hallway, followed by a scream from Casco as the knee dislocated. Bolan grabbed the wrist of the swinging arm and twisted down and in, positioning the knife blade away from his body. He then pivoted on his left foot and drove an elbow straight into Casco's temple. The knife came loose and Bolan took it from him, twisted Casco into a position so that the crime boss's spine arched backward and plunged the knife through the soft spot under his chin and drove it up into his skull to the hilt. The blade penetrated the soft palate, crunched through the sinus cavity and lodged in the forward part of the brain.

Casco's eyes widened in mixed horror and shock, and his last breath whistled oddly through his nose, a sound probably created by the metal blade sticking through his jaw and into his brain matter. Casco's body shuddered. Bolan released his hold and let Casco's twitching corpse collapse to the carpeted floor with a thump.

True to Bolan's expectations, the sound of footfalls running up the staircase alerted him to the arrival of reinforcements. Unfortunately for them, Bolan was ready. As they emerged onto the second-floor landing, the soldier brought his MP-5 K into the action, leveled it at the first hardcase to appear and triggered a short burst that drove him backward into the man following him. Both of them tumbled down the stairs, the one who'd been hit making it only halfway down before getting wedged in the staircase.

The other Los Negros soldier hit bottom, but recovered with surprising speed and reached for hardware in a shoulder holster.

Bolan neutralized the threat with a sustained burst, sweeping the muzzle across the length of the man's body and drilling him with a dozen or more rounds. Several punched through the gunman's head and blew out the back of his skull. Blood ran in deep pools from the wounds and seeped into the nearby carpet runner in the hallway.

The Executioner quickly descended the stairs and took up a ready position, prepared to meet the enemy numbers and whatever they might throw at him. Only silence ensued and as each minute ticked by, Bolan began to wonder if they were trying to deceive him. The soldier decided to sweep the house on a search-and-destroy blitz but found only empty house. For some reason, Casco hadn't seen the need to bring reinforcements. He'd kidnapped the governor of Arizona and in his own delusions he'd failed to protect the goods adequately.

Casco had committed the ultimate tactical error—he'd underestimated his enemy.

Bolan quickly placed the remaining C-4 charges in critical areas and as soon as he was clear of the house he activated the detonation switch and sent the signal. The house went up in an ear-splitting blast that would probably travel for several miles. A fireball rolled through the interior and the heat blew out every window in the house. The propane tank that supplied the house with gas went up next, and then the diesel-powered generator a moment later. And with that, the hungry flames consumed what was left of Hector Casco's reign of terror.

The Executioner made best possible speed back to where he found Governor Kampp waiting for him.

"I thought maybe you weren't coming back after all of that." She gestured at the flaming wreckage that had been Casco's house. "Is it over?"

Bolan nodded. "It's over."

Epilogue

"I'm not entirely sure I like your explanation, Brognola," Captain Joseph Hall said. "We get an anonymous call from the airport advising that Governor Kampp is safe, and then Cooper just disappears into thin air. And all you can tell me is that it's classified?"

"I'm afraid so, Captain," Brognola said. "But I'm not going to apologize for it."

"And what exactly would you like us to tell the public?"

"We gave you and Governor Kampp a more than plausible story. And you got the credit, which should do pretty good things for your career."

"Maybe so, but I have more than just the public to answer to. I've got a division supervisor along with the chief of police and mayor all asking lots of questions for which I have *no* answers."

"Well, you have quite a few friends in Governor Kampp's office," Brognola said. "She thinks you're the one to credit for Cooper's rescuing her. Pick up the phone and call in some favors."

"And that's it then?"

"You did a good job, Hall," Brognola said. "You're a good cop and you should be proud. There are a lot of very bad people off the streets of Phoenix and you're well on your way to recovering from the little crime spree the cartels had on your city. Be happy with that and keep up the pressure on the remnants."

Hall sighed. "I s'pose that's the important part. But I still feel like I'm getting stroked."

"You're not," Brognola said. "Trust me, the city's yours again. Do with that what you will but I can guarantee you won't hear any more from me unless you call for help. Cooper's broken apart the enemy's ranks. Now you've got a fighting chance."

"Well, at least pass a message on to him when you see him."

"What's that?"

"Tell him thanks. Thanks for keeping his end of the deal."

"I will. I'm sure he'll appreciate hearing it."

"Take care, Brognola."

"You, too." And then he was gone.

Captain Joseph Hall hung up the phone and turned to look out the window of his new corner office at the capitol building. As Law Enforcement Liaison to the Kampp administration, Hall found himself in a position to influence policy not just across the city of Phoenix, but through all of Arizona. He still drew his pay and order assignments from the police department—giving up his pension was out of the question after sixteen years of service—but he drew a stipend for this position and he could prioritize as he saw fit.

Hall considered what Brognola had told him, and he wondered if Cooper would ever get the message. Damn but he had to admire the hell out of the guy. Cooper had done what an entire city of highly trained and decorated police officers could not. But along the way, he'd also taught Hall that it would take more than just operating within the parameters and rules of bureaucracy. Hall had learned that it took intelligence and an ability to think like the enemy. That's why he'd already begun to establish a law enforcement exchange system between state and federal agencies and large municipalities that could call upon those resources whenever needed.

The phone rang and Hall jumped. He muttered something about getting too old for his line of work and then picked up the phone. "Captain Hall."

"I got your message."

"Cooper?"

"Yeah."

"Hey, man, I just got off the phone with Brognola. Of course, you probably knew that. Hell, you might have even been listening for all I know."

"It's always a possibility."

"Listen, Cooper, I just wanted to let you know…well, it's just…I just wanted to say thanks for everything. The governor asks about you all the time, wants to know if I've heard from you."

"Give her my regards."

"Brognola says we aren't going to see you anymore, and unless I ask for his help we probably won't hear from his side of the fence, either."

"You can stand on your own two feet now, Hall. You don't need us anymore."

"Yeah, I suppose so."

"I know so," Bolan said. "I've already heard about what you're doing to tie law enforcement intelligence assets into a unified system across the state. It's a damned good start."

"Yeah, maybe so. But we could still use about a dozen ass-kickers of your caliber."

"You'll find them. There are a lot of good men and women out there, you just have to look hard."

"Well, just the same, I'd feel better if you were around here more."

"Who knows? Maybe I'll surprise you sometime and drop in."

"You'll understand if I ask you to call ahead."

"Right."

"Say, Governor Kampp did mention if I talked to you I should let you know her door will be open as long as she's in the chair. And the same goes for me."

"Understood. But I have to go."

"On to the next crisis."

The soldier chuckled. "Something like that."

"Well, at least America will sleep a little easier tonight then."

"You can bet on it."

* * * * *

TAKE 'EM FREE

2 action-packed novels plus a mystery bonus

NO RISK

NO OBLIGATION TO BUY